INDECENT ASSAULT

A novel by

MARTYN GOFF

I0636943

VALANCOURT BOOKS

Indecent Assault by Martyn Goff
First published London: André Deutsch, 1967
First Valancourt Books edition 2014

Published by Valancourt Books, Richmond, Virginia
Publisher & Editor: JAMES D. JENKINS
20th Century Series Editor: SIMON STERN, University of Toronto
http://www.valancourtbooks.com

ISBN 978-1-939140-87-6 *(paperback)*
Also available as an electronic book.

All Valancourt Books publications are printed on acid free paper
that meets all ANSI standards for archival quality paper.

Cover by M. S. Corley
Set in Dante MT 11/13.6

for Marek Zulawski,
a great painter and a great friend,
and his wife Halina

author's note

The few people who have read this novel in manuscript have at once blamed me for one of two things: for not giving more details of the political crisis around which it centres, or for mentioning the crisis at all. I understand both objections, but my story, as the reader will discover, is concerned with a scandal on the fringe of a political situation. That it was political is incidental. Those who can remember the newspaper details vividly do not need reminders from me; the others will be more concerned, as I was, with the human passions that were at play.

There was in the fiery phantasm
a perfection which made my wild
delight also perfect, just because
the vision was out of reach, with
no possibility of attainment to
spoil it by the awareness of an
appended taboo; indeed, it may well
be that the very attraction
immaturity has for me lies not so
much in the limpidity of pure
young forbidden fairy child beauty
as in the security of a situation
where infinite perfections fill the
gap between the little given and
the great promised – the great
rose-grey, never-to-be had.

from LOLITA : Vladimir Nabokov

one

My UNCLE, you see, is a homosexual. You may wonder why I start by mentioning this, making it at once important. But then it was, for at the time of which I write my father was a cabinet minister steadily climbing the ladder to power, and already high enough for a breath of scandal to harm him. Even in these days of television and constant evening papers, only the Prime Minister, the Foreign Secretary and the Chancellor of the Exchequer are known to most people by name. The rest of the cabinet dart in and out of the news as Bills, innovations or failures are highlighted by the Press. But in a smaller circle, the tiny percentage of each community committed to political interest, there are clear shades of power and prestige between the various ministries. To the holders of those offices (and to Lobby correspondents) they are acute. That one's son was a bankrupt, one's father a confidence trickster or one's brother guilty of a homosexual crime would not call for immediate resignation or demotion. But where, as in my father's case, the competition was close, any of these things might tip the scales against him at the next reshuffle – or before.

I was twenty at the time, knowing everything, understanding little. Even what I have set down here is informed by a good deal of hindsight. I had given my parents little trouble most of the way through adolescence, not so much because I was docile or obedient, but because from an early age I had been a minor master at dissimulating my rebellion. So when my father sent for me one early September evening, I guessed that it was for another instalment of his interminable lecture on the importance of my living at home.

Most art school students find it pretty difficult to live at home. This isn't just the usual question of differences over dress or hair styles or staying out half the night. That goes for nearly all young people. But the art student has the additional thing of trying to find his creative feet in a hyperconscious world. Whereas it was once enough for him to acquire the *craft* of drawing and painting during his three years at school, now he has to stake out his position in the light of abstract or pop or op art, and be prepared for a label to be stuck on him almost before he has learnt to mix the colours. So few of us wanted to have our parents breathing down our necks, particularly as most of them thought our problems of little importance; and many of us preferred the idea of sharing a third-rate basement with a couple of other students to living at home in solitary, hemmed-in splendour.

My father nodded to me to sit. Had I at that time stopped to isolate him as a man rather than as a father, I would have termed him tall, handsome and reserved. That he was also very photogenic a thousand newspaper photographs confirm. But at the time I was only aware of him as a busy, smooth relation. I think, too, that I assumed that he was honest (for a politician), sincere (to his family and friends) and clever (which is more doubtful: I couldn't answer that with certainty to this day). He was also a stage actor/manager in the grand manner, so that even at this moment he swivelled his chair dramatically to face me, conscious – I swear it! – of the light on me, himself in the shadows, the authority of his huge roll-top desk and the warmth of his pose.

'We've understood each other too long, David, for me to waste time giving you some pi talk or other.' He took out cigarettes and offered me one. 'In any case you seem to adjust yourself to situations better than most young people, so the Royal College of Art shouldn't present you with any problems.'

I nodded, aware and amused that there was adjustment on both sides: only the slight disapproval in his tone revealed his opposition to my career.

'Morals are supposed to be pretty free there – then they were at your other art school, I believe. But you know all about unwanted babies.'

I nodded again.

'Nor did you ask me to go into politics. All the same I must rely on you to be much more discreet than the average student.' He broke off histrionically. 'A drink?'

'I could use a Cinzano, please.'

Father stood up and unlocked a cupboard by the bookcase, then continued to talk with his back to me. 'You know what I mean: a few drinks too many, and some wretched reporter's got a story about Mr Mark Coulsdon, the Minister of Communications. Soda?'

I grunted politely. I was irritated because this should all have been taken for granted, but I checked the irritation as he was probably just playing himself in.

'For some time now you have been badgering your mother and me to let you live on your own. On our side we have opposed this for a number of reasons, chief among them – as you know – that we have already made considerable concessions in the way of your career and think it only right that you should support yourself before moving away from home.' He held up his hand for silence though I had not the slightest intention of interrupting. We had had this identical conversation a dozen times. Each of their reasons for opposing my move was as illogical as the next one, and so impossible to debate.

'However, your uncle Julian, while, of course, understanding our point of view, feels strongly that now you are starting at the College it might be better for you not to live here.' He stroked his chin with the back of his hand, a gesture known to millions of televiewers at the time of the Road Act crisis. 'He has accordingly urged us to let you take the spare room in his flat, at any rate for a term or two.' He spoke faster. 'Fond of him as I am, I'm not sure he's exactly the person I would have chosen, but his very unorthodoxy might be a palliative in your eyes.' His voice tightened with embarrassment despite the cool smoking act.

I vaguely remembered Jimmy Porter on the 'Michelangelo Brigade': '. . . as if I give a damn which way he likes his meat served up,' and said: 'I don't give a damn about queers one way or the other, and Uncle Julian's rather fun.'

Father was stopped in his tracks, greasepaint, costume, the lot. He was willing to intone, with massive circumlocution, on homosexuals, coloured people or those of the Jewish persuasion, but never, if possible, to discuss them. I'd checked several dinner table harangues on the dangers of too rapid desegregation by interrupting with – 'Yes, of course, specially as there's still so much penis-envy among the whites.' At such a moment I always felt that my mother would faint if only she knew how, but she never got much further than a tiny coughing fit.

'Drink all right, David?'

'Yes, thanks.'

Then he was off again, rambling on about how I would have my own room, could come and go as I pleased, might even invite a few select friends up in the evening. I guessed that he cited that time of day since Uncle Julian's 'friend' Canter, a better-looking, less talented Kenneth-Williams-of-an-actor, was at the theatre then. While he talked I tried to weigh up the pros and cons. I desperately wanted a place of my own and had twice nearly left home to get one. At the same time my grant on its own gave me little room to manœuvre. Besides, the move to Julian would be a definite move in the right direction. I ought, I now see, to have guessed what else lay behind their sudden change of decision. But I didn't, and it's silly from this distance to pretend that I thought it was anything but a ruse to ward off a major row, leading to my leaving home altogether.

'I take it I get the same allowance?'

'Of course.' There was already relief in father's voice.

'That's something.'

'Then we can take it as settled?'

'I suppose so.'

'Good chap. You can move in any time you like between now and the beginning of term.'

I stood up. 'That all?'

Father smiled. 'About that, yes. Another drink?'

'No, thanks,' I answered firmly, and retired before I might give him the satisfaction of appearing pleased with the plan. In fact, the more I thought about it, as I climbed the stairs and shut myself in my own room, the more I liked it. First and foremost Uncle Julian was fun. He read pretty widely, knew what Pop Art stood for and thought Ella Fitzgerald great. Nor, considering his own predilection, was he likely to object to my bringing home girls from time to time. Above all he was young in mind, a trait common to the few homosexuals I had met; and this meant that one wouldn't have to be on the defensive all the time. Things like long hair (mine was), jeans (rarely off) and staying out half the night would be as natural to him as to me and my friends.

Of course there was Canter, and I didn't like Canter; nor was I sure what Uncle Julian saw in him. He was slack-limbed, effeminate, temperamental and pretty. He knew a great deal about the theatre and cinema and could talk about both subjects. But he pouted or sulked when anything else was discussed, or at least that's what he seemed to be doing; and if crossed in conversation, he would stalk out of the room, buttocks swaying from side to side. All this should have put me off; but for a reason whose logic evaded me, I was fairly sure that in any difference between the actor and me, Uncle Julian would take my side.

Our rows over my living at home had become steadily worse since the move to Belgravia. Fairly sharp things had been said on both sides, and I think my father would have given in long ago. But much as she used to deny it, my mother was excessively possessive. I can guess now that a son's leaving home symbolized once and for all her arrival at middle middle-age. At the time I just thought her bloody-minded; and I'm afraid that I said so.

Looking back to that moment when I lay on my bed and tried to work things out, I can only remember one feature that did amaze me: didn't it occur to my parents that Uncle Julian might be a dangerous influence on me? Queers are always ready to tell you that the only people they seduce in their direction are those with a predisposition to homosexuality. Myself, I doubt this. Even at twenty I knew all that jazz about everyone having a small percentage of inversion in his make-up, but I also knew that the balance could easily be tipped in the wrong direction. Perhaps my parents didn't know this, or were so sure of me that they didn't care. Only as I lay there did I begin to realize that either way they must have been very keen on my going to live with Uncle Julian.

I suppose that if I had spent the rest of the evening on my bed thinking about the situation, a number of things would have become clear. But I was not very good at working things out on my own. I needed an audience: and two nights earlier had arranged to

meet Karen at The Percolator at nine. An eighteen-year-old just
out of grammar school is not perhaps the ideal sounding-board for
tricky family problems, but no other audience was at hand. And I
was fond enough of the slim, sexy, snub-nosed girl to have almost
no inhibitions where she was concerned.

'But isn't Julian the uncle who's – ?'

'Queer, yes.'

The Percolator was fairly crowded. It had vague left-wing asso-
ciations, was used mainly by students, and accepted the French
habit, but at English prices, that one espresso gave table tenancy
for a whole evening. The owner was friendly and given to noisy
political arguing, nearly always preceding it with the 'I like to call
a spade a bloody shovel' gimmick. Despite this those of us who
wondered how he made the place pay never quite summed up the
courage to ask him.

'Is it a good thing?' Karen asked.

'Well, I won't need a pass to go in and out – nor a dress
inspection.'

'I didn't mean that.'

'What did you mean?'

Karen had the irritating habit of continuing to stir her coffee
long after all the sugar had dissolved. Eventually some of it spilt
into the saucer, and then she would look helpless until I had
collected a fresh saucer and wiped the bottom of the cup for her.
She had a lot of fairly blonde hair which covered a good deal of
her face. When embarrassed or angry she would pull it violently
back with both hands, then talk as it slipped back again. She did
this now, mercifully dropping the tired coffee spoon first.

'You don't want to get mixed up with that sort.'

'You thought Julian was rather fun when you met him.'

'His friend made me go all clammy.'

'Or doesn't my performance convince you any more?'

She softened immediately (returning, alas, to coffee stirring).
Any reference to sex between us replaced her sports car advert
look with one of tenderness. Yet she was the only girl I had ever
met who had said yes without fuss and hedging the first time I had
asked; and who never pretended that I was her first.

'Yes,' she answered softly, 'but you're worried – about going to live with your uncle. Aren't you?'

I nodded. 'I'm not sure why, either; and certainly not for the obvious reasons.'

'Some sort of prejudice?' Karen ventured. 'Oh I know, we're tolerant and sympathetic and all that. So we are with coloureds or Jews or Papists. But you wouldn't want to go and live in a house full of any of them. Or would you?'

I started to imagine it, Catholics first; then told myself they'd be the easiest of the three: occasionally unctuous, superficially moral, generally righteous. On the whole, though, they were above average, and passable company as long as they kept clear of proselytizing. Jews were similar but with different emphases. They frowned on drink, which might be inhibiting, but had an extraordinary zest for living which would be life-enhancing. Coloureds would be the trickiest. They were as human, as natural, as equal as we were, but physically too different to eliminate tension.

Karen stopped waiting. 'I had a thing with a coloured boy once.' (When? While still at school?) 'I used to go to his place, a room with a dozen others, full of negroes. They smelt differently and so did this house, and before we went to bed this acted on me like an aphrodisiac. Afterwards I found it sickly.' She stopped stirring. 'But his voice and skin and touch were so smooth – '

'And I suppose I'm as rough as a – '

'And I used to lie there and wonder: supposing he said come here and live with me. Could I do it? Would it be like being abroad among a people whose language you just couldn't learn?'

I put my hand on her arm, a little for the tenderness I felt towards her, mostly to keep her parted from her spoon. 'So you think I oughtn't to go and live with Uncle Julian?'

'No,' she answered, without looking at me. 'It might be quite a mistake.'

I tweaked her snub nose. 'You wise old thing,' I said, 'I get the message.' But it was not the one she was sending. Going to live with Uncle Julian was a challenge, in addition to anything else. And I liked challenges.

two

'People in stone houses shouldn't throw glass!'

'What's that supposed to mean?' demanded Canter, ambling into the room.

'Mr William Shepherd, Member of Parliament and hetero-sexual, should stop telling gay people what they oughtn't to do.' Julian laid down the magazine he had been reading.

In fact we had all been embarrassed long before by my uncle's flaccid attempts at humour. I had arrived at the Hampstead flat at six-thirty, brought surprisingly by my father (he had, he explained in the car, left the Ministry early for my benefit). There had been no delay, as the maid had helped me load the car during the after-noon; suitcases, books, guitar, radio, tennis racquet and a few paintings as well as two packing cases of assorted junk. The noun was mother's; most of the things in those cases had some senti-mental or intrinsic value.

Canter had never been very friendly towards me. As we dragged the things from the car, I began to wonder how the actor had received the news of my move. Had he objected? Had there been rows, followed by compromise? I had no idea on what finan-cial basis the two of them lived. Was it Uncle's flat? Did he keep Canter? And did this mean that he always got his own way? I was intrigued.

I had expected my father to leave as soon as we had emptied the car, but he accepted Julian's invitation to a drink. At once the two brothers embarked on politics, differing without quarrelling. Father was left of the Conservative centre, while Julian hovered between Labour and Liberal. Canter took no notice of them, contenting himself with finding out what films I had lately seen. Then Father left, and the three of us sat around like new boys on the first day of term. After some false starts and long silences, Julian read out pieces of his magazine while Canter darted in and out of the room (he was, I hoped, cooking some supper). Then Julian told me not to call him 'uncle' as it made him sound old; and we were more embarrassed than ever. Finally Canter told us to 'come and get it'; and we hurried to the dining-room with relief.

It was a large flat. The area between Swiss Cottage and Belsize Park still had plenty of huge Victorian houses left. Julian leased the ground floor of one of these, four large and two small rooms six steps up from the road. His hall was common to the whole house, the rest of the building being divided into six flats; and this led to a certain fussiness about the closing of doors. It took me some days to get used to this as I'm a natural door-leaver-opener, and it caused a slight tension between us. Even as I followed them into the small dining-room which faced the kitchen at the back of the house, Julian snapped: 'Shut the door after you' – pause – 'there's a good chap.'

The living-room, where we had had our drinks, was at the front of the house, its huge bay window bulging out over the basement area. Its companion, on the other side of the house, was (presumably) Julian and Canter's bedroom. I had never seen the inside of it before that night; nor had I seen the bathroom and kitchen which adjoined it. But I had been entertained in the dining-room, the small, darkly wall-papered room sandwiched between my room and the lounge. It was while I waited for them to bring in the supper that I wondered what purpose my room served in the usual way.

At once I was back on my earlier track. Did they normally have separate bedrooms? Had my coming precipitated trouble in that direction? I was not quite sure what sort of sex life queers led. I don't mean this naïvely: I had been to a boys' grammar school and had read quite a few modern novels. But whether they slept together all night like men and women or stayed together, sex or no, liked married couples, I was less sure. And thinking like this I suddenly began to realize what an unwanted trespasser I might be, forced on Canter by some piece of family blackmail outside my ken.

Julian brought in the goulash, while Canter followed with the vegetables. A good deal of fussing went on over mats, a hot plate

and serving utensils, then at last it was dished up. The stew looked
and tasted good, and once it had cooled, we ate with relish.

'Did you do this?' I asked.

Canter nodded.

'It's damn good.'

He grinned, delighted with the compliment.

'Don't make him swollen-headed,' put in Julian. 'On the other
hand it might be a good thing. As long as he's in this revue, he
thinks I ought to do the cooking.'

I glanced at my watch. 'What time are you on?'

'Not till almost nine,' replied the actor, 'and it only takes a
quarter of an hour by taxi.'

We were silent for a moment. Feeling that the atmosphere
was easier, I started: 'Look, I don't know how to put this but – or,
rather, it's a bit late, but I hope I'm not intruding – by coming
here to live, I mean.' My hesitant speech brought back some of the
tension and I wished I had postponed it.

'What *are* you talking about?' demanded Julian, putting down
his knife and fork. 'You spend three years urging me to get you
out of the home prison, then apologize when I succeed. My dear
boy, getting you to come here was the only way to work it. At the
first mention of a room of your own they behaved like outraged
Victorian grandmamas.'

Now, of course, I know that this is how my father sold the idea
to Julian. At the time I was a little put out, not knowing whether
my uncle was tactful or pleased. 'Yes, but – ' I started, waving
vaguely towards Canter.

'It's his flat,' said the actor, 'so he can do what he likes.'

Julian looked hurt.

'Yes,' I answered, only half understanding, 'but you live here,
and an extra person can be one too many.'

Canter, who had finished eating, pushed away his plate. 'Look,
duckie, if you accept us – and if you didn't you wouldn't be here –
and you don't mind our friends and frolics, you can stay as long as
you like.'

I said 'thank you' self-consciously. Next time I wanted to say
something serious, I would speak to them individually. There were

clearly sore spots I could unwittingly prod; and I had no intention of stirring up little circles of tension. I had had enough of that at home whenever my mother or I failed to realize Father's 'importance', 'overwork' or 'extreme tiredness'. Besides, I'd rather reserve my emotional overcharges for Karen and my fellow students: there would be no lack of opportunity in that direction if the College ran true to art school form.

The bell rang as they were serving the chocolate mousse. Canter had brought in the sweet while Julian cleared the table, both refusing my offer of help, Canter adding that it would be expected in the future. I had already made up my mind not to eat there often and less than ever if that evening's tension didn't dissolve (at twenty we are – or I was – impatient about everything). I am not a particularly well organized person at any time, but I began to feel that it might have been better if the three of us had had a frank conversation on daily routine before I moved in. My thoughts were cut by the arrival of two men.

'Darlings!' said Canter, splashing cream over the mousse. 'What a surprise! But I'm off in ten minutes.'

'That's why we came.'

Julian, who had opened the front door to the visitors, hurried after them into the small room. 'Find yourselves chairs, we've nearly finished. Unless you want some mousse?'

'*Do you mind!*' The taller of the two, thin, waspish, good-looking, sniffed as he spoke.

'David Coulsdon, Cy Berry, Peter Dunn.'

We all muttered and nodded to each other.

'David's come to live with us,' said Canter, with mischief.

Peter Dunn bit. '*Ménages à trois* are getting more and more fashionable.'

I was instantly indignant. Tolerance was one thing, but its extension to my being counted a member of their club was too much. Julian must have seen my face. 'David's not one of us,' he explained awkwardly; and was rewarded with a strained silence.

'The mousse is first class,' I said by way of repentance. 'Home made?'

Canter gave his mock-modest smile.

'Oh, she's a shrewd one,' said Peter Dunn, but looking at the actor, not at me.

Weeks afterwards Julian told me how embarrassed he had been that evening. It wasn't that camp chatter worried him in itself but he was anxious that I shouldn't think it was the only sort of conversation that went on in the house. At the time he said: 'You got next year's holidays fixed yet?' and everyone except me laughed.

The bell rang again. I began to feel that a party had been arranged either because of or despite me. But it was Canter's taxi, a standing order four nights a week; on the other two weekdays it came at five past two.

'We're going to Tangier with the Paddington Peters and John and Frenchy,' said Cy. 'And you?'

'Fresh talent is the spice of life,' added Peter Dunn, and we all called good night to Canter.

Coffee was served in the lounge. It was preceded by an awkward silence between the visitors and me while Julian made it. After that conversation ran like a model engine on a toy railway. Every time Julian set it firmly on the rails, one of the others knocked it off. Eventually I invented a previous date and hurried away to The Percolator.

The sight of so many normal people on the Underground gave me such pleasure that I began to suspect myself of intolerance. After all, it had surely been a compliment to me that Cy and Peter had spoken without inhibitions from the start. It did bore me after a few minutes, but the discomfort came, I think, from the feeling that Julian was ashamed. And that, from a man who had always quietly acknowledged his bent, disturbed me.

Karen was at The Percolator. At any time this might have put me out a little; in my present mood it led straight to irritability.

'I thought you were staying at home to read?'

She nodded. 'I got restless. And I thought you were staying in with Uncle?'

'Another coffee?'

'And a cake, please.'

I collected two coffees and a rich chocolate pastry, exchanging greetings with the owner and his assistant, an attractive London

University student (rumour had it that they were living together, but Karen, who knew the girl, said this was untrue). She had eyebrows pointed in the middle like Gothic arches; and was altogether a little like a Bernard Buffet portrait. Which, on thought, extended to the whole place: tall, dark-grey jugs, spiky chair legs and khaki walls. I sugared and stirred both coffees, then left the spoons on the counter.

'So I wasn't wrong after all?'

'What the hell – '

'To advise you against going to live with him.'

'What gives you that idea?'

'What else would have brought you out so quickly?'

'Oh, Karen, pack it up!'

But I was annoyed because she was right. I knew then that it was probably a mistake from my point of view; and the knowledge made me snap until we quarrelled; and quarrel until we wanted to go to bed together. Looking back over the years I find it hard to believe how much time we spent discussing possible places where we could do this. We schemed and planned, invented and dodged, and sometimes took ridiculous risks. Worse, we often ended by being uncomfortable, cold or wet. And that night the solution seemed trickier than ever.

'But why,' she demanded petulantly, 'can't we go to your room? You admit that they sleep together.'

'Oh, for crying out loud, Karen!'

She glanced round the crowded coffee bar. 'Stop shouting,' she said, making me angrier than ever. 'It seems to me you've got one standard for them and another for us. Or do you count them as married?'

She was right, of course, but I was in no mood to admit it. Society would accept our screwing with a slight qualm; Canter and Julian's with aversion or horror. Nor was I clear about the reasons for my shyness. Julian and his friend had met Karen. The room, my uncle had emphasized, was completely my own. After this evening's chatter with Cy and Peter they could hardly object to my taking anyone to bed there. But my reasoning made no headway against an inner feeling that such an action would be monstrous.

After a further bout of suggestions and vetoes we left the coffee bar, acting as if we thought that the open air might give us inspiration. But everywhere there were people and buildings and cars. Finally Karen said she had enough money for a sleazy hotel in Paddington that we had been to before. She had been saving for a new sweater but if I really wanted it so badly, we could spend it. I could hardly say 'no' without insulting her, though my desire had already lessened, and cheap hotels made it all a bit sordid. So I mustered enough enthusiasm to say 'Good girl!', then was taken aback by a placard: COMMUNICATIONS MINISTER IN NEW CRISIS. Later, from the bus I saw: COULSDON ON THE MAT WITH P.M.?, the question-mark almost illegible.

This dissolved my desire completely. I could already see the hotel manager, a fierce fat woman in my mind, challenging my false name, calling the police and revealing me as David Coulsdon, the Minister of Communication's son. Whatever it was, my father's current crisis would be dwarfed by the next day's headlines: MINISTER'S SON ON FALSE IDENTITY CHARGE. *The People*, the following Sunday, would even have found the real owner of whatever name I had appropriated: INNOCENT MAN SMEARED FOR LIFE BY MINISTER'S ART STUDENT SON.

'Penny for them?' Karen took my hand as the bus turned into the Edgware Road.

I wanted to answer: 'Let's forget the whole thing, love, and go home.' But I didn't, although she was the one girl who would not have taken offence. Or would she? 'Just wondering what Dad's been up to now.'

She frowned.

I waited for the next news-stand, then pointed to a placard.

'Evening paper froth,' she said, and, illogically, I felt better.

The hotel was just off Praed Street, one of a row of outwardly respectable Victorian houses. It was full this time, so we moved on to the next, standing in the narrow corridor to negotiate. On our right a door to the lounge was open and the television on, but the two elderly guests were watching us, not the screen. The manageress was thin, thin-lipped and supercilious.

'Stayin' the night? Two-ten in advance and sign the book.'

Karen had counselled me to argue down to the accepted £2 from whatever was quoted, but ten shillings seemed too high a price for three more minutes in that corridor. I paid, signed and felt even more embarrassment when Karen, who had wandered down the corridor, giggled loudly at a Victorian engraving. The woman meanwhile counted and re-counted the three notes, banged a key on the table and said: 'Second floor front, number twenty-two.' Then she joined the old people, straightaway becoming absorbed in a TV serial.

The room was dowdy but clean and increased my sense of self-ishness for depriving Karen of her sweater. But she was unabashed. She opened the windows, closed the curtains and took me quietly in her arms, slowly pulling me on to the bed. Ten minutes later I had forgotten about Paddington, the woman downstairs, Uncle Julian, Canter, every possible form of clothing including sweaters, and my father. At half past eleven I put Karen on the tube to Ealing where she lived with her parents, then telephoned home. My mother answered, worried at once by my late call.

'I'm all right, but what's this about Dad I saw on the placards?'

'I'm not too clear, really.' My mother's voice always sounded tired on the telephone; in the flesh she was bright and energetic. 'He said something in Committee last night that's got distorted.' She sighed. 'He's with Thompson now.'

'Thompson?'

'The Chief Whip.'

'Oh.'

'How's Uncle Julian?'

'Fine, thanks, and the room's quite good, larger than I'd imagined.'

'Good, may I have a word with him?'

I paused. 'I'm not at the flat.'

'Why not?' Her tone quickened a fraction.

'I came out to meet Karen.'

'Fancy arranging to meet her on your first night there.' She sounded disappointed.

'Well, I must get back. Tell Dad I hope it all straightens out. 'Bye.'

'Good night, David. God bless you.'

''Bye.'

I caught the tube at Marble Arch, changed, then another straight to Hampstead. The carriages were nearly empty, the few people bored or tired. Some glanced at the headlines (they still concerned my father) but most of them read the gossip columns or classified adverts. A girl with lovely legs and smart, up-to-the-minute clothes held my glance for a moment too long. It would have been easy to smile, start a conversation and arrange – well, something. But the smell of the tube, that stale, rubbishy smell, and the litter and the ceaseless, racketing noise somehow touched the same nerve as the dowdiness of the Paddington hotel, and I looked away. I let my eyes close, opening them only when the count of stopping and starting told me that it must be Finchley Road. She had gone, presumably at Swiss Cottage, and as I climbed to the road I regretted my restraint.

When I reached the flat, Cy and Peter were still there and I felt extremely weary. I would have gone straight to bed, but Julian insisted on my joining them for a nightcap. I guessed that I had been discussed in my absence, for they were more relaxed with me, though my uncle seemed otherwise on edge. We talked of the latest American musical, the Beatles (who were then becoming tremendously popular) and a new rotary electric shaver. When the visitors stood up to leave, Cy even said: 'You must bring David round one evening, Julian.'

Julian nodded and I said 'Thanks'.

'What time does Canter get in?' The three of them were nearly at the door when Peter asked his question.

'Soon,' answered Julian awkwardly.

'When the Gay Sailors Club closes,' said Cy, making as if to go but not moving.

'What do you mean?'

'Cy, that's enough!'

'But surely Julian knows?'

'Knows what?' My uncle looked anxious.

'That Canter always calls at the Club after the show.'

'Oh that – yes,' Julian replied, but it was clear that it was news.

With a last, casual wave at me they left the room. I stood, ready to go to bed as soon as Julian came back. Once more I was puzzled by what I had heard. Mildly malicious gossip is not a prerogative of homosexuals: it's common in all walks of life. But it had been clear from the moment of my return that the three of them were in an easy, friendly mood; and Cy had been pleasantly entertained for a whole evening (there were two lots of dirty glasses and some plates that must have had sandwiches or cakes on them). Yet his item about Canter had been carefully timed and introduced.

Julian poured himself another drink on returning, then sat on the long, black sofa. I was still standing. 'I do wish he wouldn't tell lies,' he said feelingly. 'You know, David, we've been together eight years and I can't cure him of this blasted lying. It goes on and on and on . . .'

His tone, and the jealousy that inspired it, opened up a whole segment of homosexual affairs that had never existed for me until then. 'I am sorry,' I mumbled.

'And so am I,' answered Julian, his mood changing. 'I meant this evening to show you how very ordinary we were, instead of which . . .' He grinned boyishly. 'Perhaps that's just what it has done.' He lifted his glass to me.

three

GRANDFATHER Coulsdon was a successful carrier in the days when Carter Patterson was a small firm. He had two sons and a daughter. Mark, the older boy, followed him into the business, shared in the compensation when it was nationalized, then devoted himself to politics. Muriel, the daughter, married Richard Garstein, the music critic, and largely disappeared into the world of 'The Garden', Glyndebourne and the Festival Hall. Julian, the youngest, became an accountant, won a DSO in the war and emerged from the Air Force to become a stockbroker, achieving a partnership at the same time as Mark became a Junior Minister. When Grandfather Coulsdon died, his children had all attained some degree of success. He was even able to cheer his own departure by predicting that Mark would be Prime Minister one day.

This much I had known before I moved to my uncle's flat. There, sometimes at breakfast, sometimes late at night, I began to fill in the details. I learnt how Julian had come to terms with his inversion, leading a clear-cut double life until he had met Canter, then gradually allowing the private to overflow into the public sector. Business associates began to be invited to dinner; Canter was included in return invitations. What had been permissible only with the Raptons, now became the norm with a wide range of friends and acquaintances.

The Raptons came to dinner during the week following my arrival in Hampstead. Since the unhappy start I had eaten out every night, returning late partly to avoid further gatherings, partly in the hope of meeting the girl who had caught my eye in the tube. Meanwhile, details of the relationship between Julian and Canter began to come into focus. Odd, shouted remarks, raised eyebrows and spiked kidding revealed their particular tensions. Canter, somewhat financially and altogether emotionally dependent on Julian, was still very promiscuous. This hurt my uncle until he accused the actor of a whole range of sins from ingratitude to immorality. The morning of the Raptons' visit had provided one such row, clearly audible through closed doors.

'Are you doing anything tonight?' Julian asked, appearing in my doorway before leaving for the City.

Ordinarily I would have said 'yes', but he looked defeated and forlorn; and I had heard Canter accusing him of trying to 'buy love', so I shook my head.

'Do join us for dinner, then: our friends the Raptons are coming. He's a publisher and she's a sociologist, and I've known them for donkey's years.'

'OK.'

He raised his black, initialled briefcase in greeting, then hesitated. 'I hope our little tête à tête didn't disturb you?'

I shook my head again. Uncle Julian had always been jolly and carefree. Since living there I had found him mainly vulnerable.

'Good. See you.' This time he went, but I was not to be left in peace. Canter, in black pyjamas and red dressing-gown, knocked on my door five minutes later. He looked tired and sheepish.

'May I come in?'

I nodded.

'Julian ask you to stay in tonight?'

'Yes.'

'And?'

'I said "yes" – thank you.'

Canter spun the tassel at the end of his dressing-gown cord. 'You'll like the Raptons. Even I have to be on my best behaviour.'

'I thought,' I said, watching him as his eyes made an inventory of my pictures and other effects, 'I thought they knew the score?'

Canter laughed. 'You're catching our lingo,' he said, 'what *fun*! You'll be mincing next.' He sat on the bed, which was still unmade. 'Mind? They do, but no one ever says anything. "What people do in bed is their own business," says Molly, "and I wish they'd keep it that way." And Lance publishes a gay novel every four or five years but tells us he's not had time to read it.' The actor scratched himself between the legs. 'How long you staying?'

I had been sitting at the table sketching when he arrived. Now I swung round. 'Is that an invitation to leave?'

Canter stared back. 'It would be if it was my flat.'

'At least that's honest,' I thought for a moment. 'I'll see if I can be out by the end of the week.'

'Without telling Julian I put you up to it?'

I stood. 'Look, chum, what's going on? If you want me to go I'll go, but two can play at the honesty racket. If I go, Julian will certainly know – '

'Forget it!' His tone had changed dramatically from spite to appeal. 'I didn't really mean it anyway. It's just that you're always judging us – and condemning, judging and condemning, though it's not surprising considering what we are, is it?'

'I suggest we cut the self-pity,' I answered, sitting down again, annoyed that I had momentarily let him get under my skin. I ought to have recognized from the start that he was playing for sympathy.

'It's easy for you to talk.' He lay back on the bed. 'When you whistle at a girl in the street, you don't get arrested. When you're tired of sleeping round, you can get married and have a wife and a home and kids.' He sat up again and stared at me. 'Not that I want that, of course – but I wish I did. Anyway, I'm wasting your precious time, and you're probably wanting to go out.'

The pause made the statement a question. As he pulled himself languidly off the bed and ambled to the door, the conversation fell into place: he wanted me to move out of the flat because he entertained people there in the mornings. I regretted the thought, but it was true just the same. 'I've got some work to do first,' I said casually, and the disappointment on his face confirmed my suspicion.

'When's the term start?'

'At the college? Monday week.'

Canter opened the door. 'By the way – though you'll see this for yourself – Molly Rapton's madly in love with Julian.' He waited for my reaction (and I must have looked surprised), then sidled into the corridor with a tired wave. 'Don't overwork,' he called behind him.

At seven that evening Julian and Canter came into the living-room together. Both wore dark blue, mohair suits, my uncle's set off by a white shirt, the actor's by a blue one. With their suits they had donned new personae. As he checked the cocktail cabinet, Julian told a couple of jokes he had heard during the day; gave us an amusing sketch of one of his senior partners; and mimicked a man who had made a speech to all and sundry after being put on the wrong train by a coloured porter. Canter, camp manner-isms cut to a minimum, played aloof, laughing good-naturedly at the jokes and tidying the room in a vague, almost masculine way. Then he went out to get some nuts.

'There's just one thing,' started Julian as the door closed behind the actor, 'the Raptons weren't always C of E.'

'What's that to do with – '

'He's a convert from Judaism.'

'Why the need to warn me?'

'He's touchy on that – and allied subjects.'

'Couldn't have been done with great conviction?' I suggested.

'With none,' answered Julian, delighted with his enigma. 'He comes from one of those top-level Jewish families, Conscience-of-the-Rich class.' He paused to see if I took the point.

'Lewis Elliot's been there, too.'

He smiled. 'But Lance never felt he was a Jew.'

'*Lance?*'

'Lionel Rappaport, if you must. The only thing was that the world didn't agree with him. His father was Solomon, his mother Rebecca and their circle Jewish.'

'So to get rid of the label, he sewed in another?'

'You're quick on the uptake, David.'

I found it extraordinary that people should so recklessly commit themselves to a double life. After all, according to most theories Canter and Julian had no choice: they were either born queer or slanted that way by environment. But surely one didn't have to become a Protestant to deny one was a Jew. 'So now he's got a two-way guilt complex?'

The bell answered instead of Julian. The story had disposed me against the guests, and I was more sorry than ever that I had not pleaded another engagement. What the hell hope was there

for anyone who couldn't be honest in religion and sex? And if he
was such a coward, what point was there in my spending a whole
evening with Lance Rapton and his wife?

The first few minutes after their arrival told me clearly what I
could do with my prejudices. By my standards Julian was quite a
good-looking man. I was to learn in those few months that queers
have a different code of assessment. To them a man's looks are
bound up with a scale of sexual attraction that ranges from the
soft and blond to the rugged and dark. To me a man is handsome if
he has a good bone-structure, balanced features and an open face.
Julian had all that, heightened by thick, greying hair and a long,
noble nose. But beside Lance Rapton he seemed ordinary.

The publisher was almost a cliché for the models used in rugged,
outdoor advertising: tall, well-built and handsome. He stayed with
the cliché by having a quick, friendly smile and warm manner, and
departed from it in details that became apparent as time went by.
Once, when he was listening to his wife telling a story that superficially showed him in an embarrassing light, I noticed something
furtive in his look. Just as, when you are first shown an unnoticed
flaw in a familiar painting, you can never disregard it again, so
Lance from then on always had something sly about him. He was
also, despite his friendliness, slightly aloof in a patronizing way.

I had no early reservation about his wife. Molly looked a young
middle-aged woman who had dieted sharply, but with attractive
results. Her head and build seemed too large for the thin, comfort-
ably dressed person who greeted me, but turned away to fuss over
Julian. This, and many later moments, bore out Canter's surprising
charge, though looking from Lance to Julian, it was hard to understand it.

'What branch?' Lance asked, when Julian told him that I was
going to the Royal College.

'Painting.'

'All this pop stuff?'

'That's a reactionary remark for a liberal publisher,' said Julian,
handing Lance a whisky.

'Since when is my dear husband a liberal anything?' Molly raised
her glass to Julian. 'Except in money, of course.'

I was relieved that we had so quickly slid off a superficial conversation about my career and/or modern art. Simultaneously my
hopes for the evening were lowered. Casual kidding was obviously
going to step in whenever the talk threatened to become serious.
Now I don't mind this when I'm with people of my own age, but
if I've got to spend an evening with the elderly I want something
more solid. So while Canter withdrew to the kitchen, I studied the
professional way in which the small talk was patted back and forth;
and was quite unready for Lance's: 'Well, young David, and what
are the chances of your old man becoming PM one day? Mark you,
he only just missed shaving off his bumpers altogether the week
before last if I'm not mistaken.'

I suppose most people think it must be fun or an advantage to
have a father who is a celebrity. It gives you a certain amount of
glamour; and if you lack your own or prefer a brighter, reflected
variety, it could be an advantage. But I don't. Then again, whether
your father's a millionaire or a Cabinet Minister, it can be a pass to all
sorts of places and circles. Even in adolescent society, membership
of clubs, groups, fraternities and the like is easier for the boy with a
prominent parent. And slightly reluctant girls are sometimes more
ready to go to bed with the offspring of an Important Man than
with John Smith's son. Before I add that none of this counted with
me, I must admit that most people use their relatives and friends in
one way or another. So my refusal to trade on my father's success
was partly illogical, partly the feeling that it was too strong a trump
to be used indiscriminately. On the other hand I tried not to resort
to the attitude that pretended ignorance of him and his position.

'The odds are against,' I replied slowly. 'He's only three years
younger than Corner who's the white-haired boy at the moment,
and a few years older than Bradley who's much cleverer anyway.'

'Shame!' This came from Julian in an indulgent tone.

'Well, it's true,' I insisted. 'Of course there's still the little question of luck.' I hesitated. 'Dad's a pretty good PRO for himself,
and there's another thing: if Corner and Bradley tie for the job,
it might have to go to someone else. Still, all that's years away. Sir
Brian's only sixty-four, which everyone keeps telling me is young
these days.'

In the corner by the window Molly started to talk softly to Julian. 'I understand he won't lead the party in the next Parliament,' said Lance.

I resented the publisher's tone: 'The party' meant 'our party'. Julian must have heard this out of one ear. 'David's Labour,' he called across the room.

Lance addressed me directly in reply. 'It's like measles and mumps in childhood,' he opined. 'Pretty inevitable, but you'll soon get over it. Still,' he went on, making it clear that he expected no denial, 'your old man's going to have to mind his p's and q's. Another slur on the little man in his Sunday mini – however true it is – and he'll be rated a liability instead of an asset.'

Julian left the room to go to Canter's help.

'Who will?' Molly asked as she joined me on the divan.

'His father, if he doesn't watch his step.'

I didn't like Lance's tone. 'The lot of us, if it comes to that. Me, Mother, even Julian.'

'Julian!' Molly was angry. 'He has absolutely nothing to do with your father's career. Not that he's ever likely to do anything that would hurt anyone.'

'I wouldn't be so sure,' said her husband.

'What do you mean by that, Lance?'

He waved his arm round the room, at the same time giving me a conspiratorial wink. 'This sort of set-up's normal enough to people like us, but it's really only accepted by the upper ten per cent.'

'They seem to live quietly enough,' I put in, watching myself being edged into the position of defender.

'I'm not so sure about Canter,' said Molly.

'Meaning?'

I tried to stave off any revelations or guesses. 'He's very loyal.'

'And promiscuous,' said Molly firmly, 'at least so I hear.'

The publisher frowned. 'Where do you get this sort of gossip from?' He paused for an answer. When none came, he added: 'From Julian?'

She was saved from the need to answer by my uncle's return. He told us that dinner was served and that we should bring our drinks to the dining-room. Molly obeyed with alacrity, taking Julian's arm as she went through the door. Lance started to follow then turned back to me. 'The truth is, you know, David, that politicians need bright wives and conventional families.'

'And no art students among their children?'

Before he could answer, Julian shouted for us from the dining-room. 'Coming,' I called, but Lance held me back. He spoke very quietly: 'I'm an old friend of your uncle's you know. What I'm going to say is not disloyal to that friendship, though you may think so at first. But don't you think you're exposing your father to unnecessary danger by living here? You heard what Molly said about Canter, didn't you? I'd heard the same thing myself more than once.'

The door was thrown back. 'What's going on between you two?' asked Julian with a smile. 'We're all waiting for you.'

We mumbled our apologies and followed him to the dining-room.

four

I was almost sorry for Canter when he had to leave without his sweet, but his departure changed the tone of the evening. It was not that he had behaved in a camp or flamboyant way, dominated the conversation or disturbed the rest of us by inattention. On the contrary he had been a serious, attentive host. But once his taxi had carried him off to the theatre, Julian's intellectual stature seemed to increase, Molly stopped flirting with him and Lance shed some of his portentous manner. The publisher also stopped condescending to me. When the conversation turned to abstract art, he even listened to what I had to say.

As we sat drinking coffee back in the drawing-room, I wondered whether the atmosphere would change again when Canter returned. I was fairly sure that he would give his club a miss that evening, knowing that the Raptons would still be at the flat. Here, however, I was wrong. After two hours of foreign holidays, some books Lance was publishing and one of those brief, unrewarding exchanges about current West End plays, Molly said it was time to go.

'Canter should be back in a few minutes,' said Julian, smiling hopefully. 'Curtain came down half an hour ago.'

Molly was already on her feet. 'Give him our love and say we thought the dinner delicious.' She put her hand on Julian's shoulder. 'But we must go. Lance is off to Wales early in the morning to see a glamorous novelist he keeps there.'

'I'll say!' agreed the publisher, getting slowly to his feet. 'She's seventy-nine, or maybe it's eighty, next birthday. But as she continues to sell thirty thousand per book, I have to look after her.'

In the hall mutual friends were discussed. The Raptons indulged in some lightly malicious gossip that they wrapped in the convention of to know all is to forgive all. I stood in the drawing-room doorway listening and smiling as required, but conscious that there was little difference between this and the parting shots of Cy and Peter on my first evening there. Then a tenant from one of the upper floors let himself in, the group stood aside to let him pass and the mood was broken. After a few quick kisses and handshakes the Raptons left. Julian and I went back to the drawing-room.

'Drink?'

I nodded though I had drunk a good deal already. I was hardly tipsy or very merry, but I was beyond the stage of saying 'no'. I sensed, too, that Julian was going to pour out his heart, and the size of the drink he gave me confirmed my suspicion. I found that I no longer cared. I was becoming increasingly certain that he was being ill-used by Canter: in my present mood I would provide sympathy or advice as necessary, particularly if I could pay the actor back for his attempt to push me out.

'What did you make of them?' asked Julian, throwing his leg over the arm of the chair.

'They're rather an unusual couple.'

'And nice?'

'I'm not sure about him.'

'You mustn't be put off by his – ' Julian stopped at the sound of a car door slamming. When no footsteps followed, he went on: 'I do wish he could have made the effort to get back just this evening. Lance and Molly are sensitive to that sort of thing.'

I was only partly relieved by the change of subject. 'Has this been going on long?'

Julian nodded. 'It's like a drug to him. The more he has, the more he needs to get the same satisfaction.' He sighed. 'The colossal vanity of it all.'

I was lost. 'Vanity?'

'Yes, vanity. He wants flattering hourly. It's become so bad that he loses his sense of identity without it. Everything hinges on his beauty and youth and ability to conquer.' He stopped abruptly. 'You thought it was sex *qua* sex he was after?'

I nodded.

'No, not a bit of it. Of course, it often slides into that before he can stop it, but he doesn't enjoy it that much. He prefers sex in the head to the real thing.'

I wondered whether this was true or just a defence that Julian employed to himself. I wondered, too, whether he felt that it gave him the right to have his fun on the side; but I couldn't bring myself to ask that sort of question – yet. Instead I said: 'You're still pretty fond of him, I gather, so it must be rather painful for you?'

Julian sat up. 'Yes and no, by which I mean that sometimes it is and sometimes it isn't. Some nights I'll go off to bed without caring a straw what he's doing and hardly wake when he comes in. Others – well, I start thinking, thinking of Canter and me as we were and dreaming of what we still might be. And I get wider and wider awake.' He looked at me shrewdly for a moment. 'Then I begin to get bitter, you know, wish him dead or maimed or in a taxi crash. Until he comes in, and I'm relieved. The funny thing is that it doesn't stop me picking a quarrel and we almost invariably end with an almighty row.'

'I see.' His little account illuminated a number of conversations and actions that I had witnessed in the flat.

'Do you? Or are you wondering why I go on at all? If you are, then I haven't got the answer to that one. Love? Too overlaid by now to be sure. Sense of responsibility? Strong, but you can't go on being someone else's keeper for ever, can you? Fear of loneliness? That, too, probably.'

I had always admired Julian; now I began to be sorry for him. The carefree, with-it, eternally young man was a party persona. Behind it lay the old, old story of lack of love, of loneliness and of the fear – yes, Canter's fear, but in more subtle form – of age and decline. The very qualities that I had admired were shallow against the defect. I felt sorry for Julian – and liked him a little less.

'What was Rapton whispering to you before dinner?' he asked suddenly.

I had no sense of loyalty to the publisher. 'His fears that a scandal connected with you might damage Dad's career.'

'He's right!'

I was surprised. 'But, Julian – '

'No!' He got up to pour himself another drink. 'I gathered you didn't like Lance much, and I'm sorry. At your age one is easily put off by people who are patronizing and condescending, and Lance is both. But he's a lot of other things, too.' He sat down again, cocking one leg over the arm of the chair as before. 'He's on a host of committees and boards, none of them paying as much as expenses, and only a few of them in any way glamorous. He likes power and plays for it, but in return he gives twenty times as much as most people. And despite his languid manner, he's got a tremendous amount of drive and energy.'

'From his Jewish origins, no doubt?'

Julian straightened in the chair. 'Yes,' he replied in a tone that suggested that I was making an anti-semitic remark.

He let his head drop. Each hour that evening had seemed to add two or three years to his age, and now he looked as firmly middle-aged as my father. In those days I accepted things at their face value more easily than I would now. Julian had said that he had come to terms with his inversion; and his claim seemed justified. With my present knowledge of the world I would have looked beyond what I was told to where I would have recognized the cost to anyone of living outside society's normal frontiers.

'Poor Canter,' said Julian at length. He shook his head sadly, then, unprompted, started a long dissertation on the actor. He had been born into a poor, artisan family. While his father (now dead) had been a weak man forever oppressed by employers, landlords and *them*, his mother (still alive) had dominated the family from the day of their marriage. There were three other children, all boys, and she had forced each of them up at least one social or commercial rung. For her fourth child she had wanted a daughter, but had taken her disappointment well, spoiling and petting him as she had none of the others. As a result Canter (his real name, it now came out, was Fred!) had been envied and resented by the rest of the family, including his mild-mannered, diminutive father.

At school he had filled in the pattern laid down for him: good at English and History, outstanding as a mimic and amateur actor, poor in everything else. He had been removed early and put to work in a men's outfitters, graduating in a few years to a boutique of the smarter kind. There he had met a producer who didn't want to go to bed with him, but who just the same offered him a small part in a revue. Julian had encountered Canter at a stage party three revues later (he had gone as Cy's guest); and after two weeks the actor had left home to come to Hampstead.

'At first it was what Canter used to call "socko". I was pretty keen on him physically and he wanted my sort of older, protective love. And there were the struggles to hold us together. His mother disapproved of me and his leaving home in about equal proportions; and she didn't just leave it at disapproval. Your mother was horrified. She even went as far as inviting one of my partners for drinks to try to wheedle him into warning me. Not that either side said anything openly. Disparity of ages, social backgrounds, careers, even working hours, were all mentioned, but never a breath of the only thing that was in their minds. And this held us together, as you can imagine. We felt – ' he laughed in his old carefree way – 'we were fighting the world for *the love that dares not speak its name!*'

He rose ponderously to pour himself another drink, but his voice and expression remained mocking. 'This particular cold war went on for some time, but in the end we won. Canter's father died and – this is quite uncanny, David – all the struggle went out of his old woman. She even started to come over to wash our shirts. And your mother and father just gave up. At the same time I cooled off Canter, at least at the physical level, and his minor theatrical successes lessened his needs for a father-protector.' He sat down abruptly. 'And that's where we are now, only a bit more so.'

Some of the pieces fitted; others didn't. 'So why do his goings-on still hurt?'

Julian ran the tip of his finger round the rim of his glass. 'I don't know. There's probably more love left than I'm willing to allow. You can't measure these things in a routine way. It's only when someone wants to leave you or is hurt or killed that you know – much too late! – how much feeling there was all the time.'

I felt that I was entitled to my question now; or perhaps the last large drink had dulled another inhibition. 'And do you also have friends – on the side?'

Julian's demeanour altered so sharply that even now I feel that I must have exaggerated the change. Whereas he had been sad and self-mocking by turns, he became melodramatic. He stood, sat

down, stood again and strode about the room. Looking back over
the years, I realize that he felt deeply and was keen that I should
understand this, even if it meant acting his case. On the evening in
question I just thought he was being histrionic, indulging one of
the sides of the typical queer that I don't like.

'If only it was as easy as that,' he started, then broke off to stare
at me. 'Mind you, David, I'd be perfectly honest if I gave you a
straight "no!" in reply. Perfectly. But that would only answer the
question you've asked.' He stopped for his glass. 'There's another
question you wouldn't know about.'

I was at sea now. Did he mean that he had another full-time
lover on the side? Or that he was carrying on with Molly Rapton?
He had been warm and charming with her, but there had been
no hint of his returning her obviously sexual approaches. Then
what could the question be? For a moment I wondered whether
he meant me to ask if he were impotent. Julian impotent? I wasn't
really sure if and how one could distinguish who was, but he
seemed so virile and energetic that I ruled it out.

When he started to supply the answer of his own accord, his
voice had changed again. The tone was even, lacking both its usual
bounce and its recent melodrama. 'Fifty years ago a referendum on
changing the law about queers would have produced something
like ninety-five per cent no's. But a couple of wars, the Wolfenden
Report, programmes on the telly and the Reverend Sherwin Bailey
have altered that.'

'Sherwin Bailey?'

Julian pointed to one of the bookshelves. 'The chap who wrote
Homosexuality and the Western Christian Tradition or some such
title. He shows that our attitudes mainly derive from the story
of Sodom and Gomorrah. And then goes on to explain that Lot's
boys were not queer at all. The whole thing turns on the trans-
lation of one verb from Hebrew to Greek.' He paused. 'I bet you
didn't know that?'

I agreed.

'Well, what with one thing and another, today's referendum
might be fifty-fifty, but – ' he wagged a finger at me – 'only for what
I call straight queers, adults who stick to adults, operate in private

and keep quiet about what they do in bed. For the rest it's still the Inquisition.'

'The rest?' I was simultaneously fascinated and irked by my fascination.

'The rest,' repeated Julian. 'My particular brand is young boys. Oh yes, I may have had a lot to drink but I can still see the look on your face, the sheer bloody horror of it. And don't start on me. I know it's wrong, evil, sinful, the lot. I know that you *may* corrupt a kid for life, change him – pervert him. But knowing all that doesn't stop me wanting to put my hand round his little waist or stroke his tight, rounded little bottom.' He stopped abruptly. 'Of course, I've never done it, never touched a single golden hair of a single golden boy. Just stood and watched – and stamped on my bloody toes to keep me rooted to the pavement.' He slumped in the chair, banged his glass on the table and stared at the wall. 'So that was the question you didn't ask, David. But you'll be full of disgust just the same.'

I opened my eyes widely. 'Why the hell do you and your sort imagine we care all that much either way? Hasn't anyone told you about the Bomb or people starving in India? One little boy more or less in this or that camp isn't going to upset any real applecart. If people like you make me sick, it's not for the reasons you think.'

Julian got to his feet. He looked suddenly sober. 'I'm terribly sorry, David,' he started with a new humility. 'I suppose that's what comes of bottling things up for so long.' We both started as the front door slammed. 'Not a word to Canter, I need hardly add.'

I nodded my head in agreement as the actor came into the room.

five

I THINK I told Karen about Julian because I was dissatisfied with my reaction to his story. His self-pity had anticipated the lurid horror only possible to an elderly Victorian; yet I ought to have been slightly shocked all the same. Here was a nominally decent, moderately successful man confessing a repulsive and irresponsible perversion. That Julian would have been indistinguishable in a middle-class crowd made it worse: we like our villains to act and dress the part. Yet all I could experience in face of his confession was mild fascination, mild boredom and a mild wish that I had never joined the household in the first place.

'Well?' I demanded when Karen remained silent. We were in the Percolator. It was full of 'strangers' that evening and we resented them. After all, didn't we call it *our* coffee bar?

She was stirring her coffee. 'I'm getting rather sick of the whole subject,' she said quietly. 'Can't we talk about something else?'

'Such as?'

She laid down her spoon and put her hand on mine. 'Us. Or the world. Or your father.'

'OK,' I replied, feeling the snub but knowing that she was right. 'So what have you been doing since I last saw you?'

'Rowing with the family as usual.'

'About?'

'Being on the dole. Seriously, David, are women ever on the dole?' She picked up her spoon again. 'I've got to get a job.'

'I thought you were waiting to see whether you got into art school first?'

'So did I, but Mummy says I've got to get a job until the other comes through. If it does.'

'Cheer up,' I said.

Before she could say anything further we were joined by two regulars. They arrived discussing a new folk group and were soon

41

drawn into the argument. Then one of them stopped the conversation by telling us of a folk festival in Antibes the following June.
Couldn't the four of us go together, hitching and scrounging our
way across France? In the next half hour, with eight months still
to go, we made detailed plans for the trip. Then Roger and his girl
friend left us as quickly as they had come.

'I don't think I like her,' said Karen thoughtfully. 'He's fab.'

'Thank you.'

'Don't mention it.'

'If you didn't like her why were you so keen on this foursome
thing?'

'So we can go to France together.'

'You're nuts. Anyway, what job are you going to do?'

As usual Karen treated the question upside-down. She would
refuse to be a secretary or work in a shop or be a doctor's recep-
tionist. When I protested that this excluded her from ninety-five
per cent of available posts, she retorted that she had two good 'A'
levels.

'So?'

'I wouldn't mind training as a probation officer or – '

'*You?*' I snorted. 'Besides, what happens if the call comes from
an art school?'

'Well, something to do with helping people and that sort of
thing, then.'

I could think of nothing for a few moments, then I had a brain-
wave. 'Listen, Karen. The other evening Julian and Canter had a
couple to dinner. He was a la-di-da, patronizing publisher, but she
was quite pleasant – and a sociologist. Supposing I could arrange
for you to meet her?'

'You mean to get some advice?'

'Yes.'

Karen was so delighted with the idea that we spent the rest of
the evening discussing my problems. Since my behaviour at the
time of the scandal was affected by them, it might be as well to
mention them at this stage, though I have already hinted that they
mainly arose from my career at art school. While I must have
seemed an averagely integrated person to the outside world, I was

going through a small crisis that reduced other people's troubles to academic interest. At school I had shown a certain small brilliance as a painter. Grammar schools are not great fomentors of artistic talent, but some of them, mine included, have brilliant art masters. I had gone to a local art school with a good reputation and a dozen exciting canvases; I had moved on with the reputation only. Whatever I now tried to do seemed to be hollow: everyone had already done or tried it before. I vacillated between the semi-abstract and representational schools, feeling in both that I was only paying lip service. And this failure to connect, to establish myself in my own right, had begun to worry me. Was the whole thing a mistake as a career? Ought I to cut my losses and do something else? I was confused and not really in the mood to worry about my uncle's or anyone else's problems. Only for Karen's difficulties could I show more than polite interest.

So I arranged for her to meet Molly Rapton. Julian gave me her telephone number, though he was dissuaded with difficulty from giving a small party to bring Molly and Karen together. Molly herself seemed delighted by my call, but I had to accede to drinks instead of the simple meeting I had foreseen.

The Raptons lived in Hampstead in a large Georgian house overlooking the Heath. I don't care much for antiques and so know little about them. The large, well-proportioned rooms may have been furnished with reproduction or the real thing: certainly they looked opulent, grand and intimidating. (I have a private theory that people who grow up in small rooms yearn for riches to have big ones; and vice-versa. I feel exposed in huge libraries and drawing-rooms, secure in 'dens' and bed-sits) And Molly received us from a deep armchair, less relaxed and more *grande-dame* than at Julian's.

'Lance isn't back yet. He's bidding for some frightful American novel and was afraid the call would come through while he was on his way if he didn't wait for it.'

We sat, looking, I suppose, a bit lost. Karen's hair was long and slightly unkempt, her sweater too obviously mine and her skirt her mother's. I had put on a suit.

'He hasn't reached the stage of having a phone in his car yet?'

Molly shook her head and laughed politely. 'How's Julian?

'They're both fine.'

The Spanish maid brought in another couple. Robert Standsfield was a stockbroker, his wife a smart Belgravia hostess. At the introductions I was a little sharp, irritated at Molly's turning the occasion into a social event. How many people were coming, I wondered. It looked as though we would have to leave as soon as possible.

'David's Julian Coulsdon's nephew,' Molly said as everyone began to sit down again.

'Really? You in stockbroking, too?'

'He's an art student,' Molly explained for me.

'Where?' It was Mrs Standsfield's turn. Nor did she wait for an answer. 'You must come along to one of my Tuesday *salons*. I know just how exciting it is for you young painters to meet the famous.' She spun off five established names. 'Of course they don't all come every week, but you'll soon meet them bit by bit.'

'How marvellous,' said Karen suddenly and unexpectedly, while I was coping with the image of a roster for great painters.

'Do you paint as well?'

Karen shook her head. 'But I want to – or at least I want to study design.'

The conversation was going the wrong way. If Molly was made to feel that sociology was an also-ran, she would be slow to help. 'Karen's rather torn between that and going in for something like probation work or helping old people,' I said firmly. 'In fact we were rather hoping that Molly might have some bright ideas.'

Lance's arrival changed the subject. He apologized for being late and told of his continuing battle for the rights of the American novel. Then he asked Mr Standsfield about the state of some shares he had recently bought; and the company split into two. Being geographically nearer the men, Karen listened to their conversation while I faced the two women.

'Your father seems to have recovered his form,' Mrs Standsfield started. 'At least I assume he's your father.'

Molly agreed for me, then added: 'You mean on TV last night?'

'Yes. I thought it was the best party political broadcast for some time. Didn't you?'

'Actually,' I said, 'I didn't see it. I didn't even know he was on, I'm afraid.'

'David's living with Julian at the moment.'

Mrs Standsfield glanced at Karen then at me, then back at Karen. 'Is that actor fellow still there?'

'Yes,' I said, 'he is. Don't you like him?'

Mrs Standsfield cut across Molly's *sotto voce* 'Who does?' with: 'He never really registers where I'm concerned. Only Julian gets so hurt if you don't invite them together.'

'He's very good-looking,' I suggested, 'and quite amusing at times.'

'What do you want me to do for Karen?' demanded Molly.

'I thought you might tell her how to get into this sociology racket – or at least whether she's got any chance at all.'

Molly thought for a moment. 'I think it would be more sensible if she came to see me for a coffee one morning.'

I nodded tamely, amazed at the complicated stratagems women evolve. If Karen was to be invited back alone, what were we doing there for drinks? The Standsfields already knew Julian, so my being the Minister of Communication's son could hardly be the reason; while at Julian's Molly had only been politely friendly. Puzzled, I turned to rescue Karen: 'Learning how to get rich quick?'

Mr Standsfield broke off a little speech he was making. 'How very rude of me, my dear,' he said to Karen, then turned to face the room. 'Do you know the Marcus Levys? We had dinner with them last Monday. Nice people, but whenever one of their precocious little children came into the room, they broke off the conversation and devoted their whole attention to the wretches.' He narrowed his eyes. 'It's strange, you know, but there's always something *nouveau riche* even with the most assimilated of that race.'

'Who's Marcus Levy?' asked Lance, his voice cold.

'The Furniture King. Head of Guardian Furnishings. Very shrewd, and very dynamic. Quite friendly, too, and yet like the rest of that tribe, he keeps you at a distance.'

'But isn't that what the Jews say about us?' Karen's voice was too loud.

'What do you mean, my dear?'

'Well, Jews are always so warm and friendly,' she emphasized firmly. 'And they find middle and upper-middle English stand-offish. I had a Jewish girl-friend at school, Rebecca Myers, and her father was always grumbling about that. "You can send your boy to Harrow and Oxford," he used to say, "and get him into all the right Clubs, but he'll never be one of them."' She laughed. 'He used to say it with such an air of resignation that I always wanted to cheer him up.'

There was silence then. It wouldn't have surprised me to learn that the Standsfields thought Karen a Jewess: her outburst had been so opposed to Mr Standsfield's message. Molly opened her mouth then changed her mind, rotating her lower jaw as if quietly exercising it. Lance said nothing, though I guessed that he was waiting for the chance to change the conversation.

'Do you think Jews are ever completely assimilated?' I asked him.

'I've never really given the question much thought.' His tone was off-hand, but there was a definite appeal for help when he turned to Molly. 'I don't think we've got any Jewish friends, have we, darling?' He gave a short, deprecating laugh. 'Not that we've ever tried to arrange it that way.'

'Aren't the Carnes Jewish, at least by birth?' The innocence in Molly's tone was also perfectly calculated.

'I thought you had some Jewish blood in you somewhere, Lance?' Mrs Standsfield turned to her husband. 'Who told us that, dear?'

Mr Standsfield looked irritated. 'Marcus said he'd heard –' He let his voice tail off, then shrugged his shoulders.

'Have you?' asked Karen brightly.

Lance was too slow in answering. A quick 'no!' would have been accepted by everyone except me; a dismissive 'yes', implying perhaps one grandparent, would have kept him clear of Mr Standsfield's rating. His 'I think most of us are pretty mixed if it comes to that' convinced no one, even though it was delivered in an easy languid way.

'I wish I had,' said Karen stubbornly.

I admired her persistence, but thought that now, perhaps, it was a little unfair to go on punishing her victim.

'Why?' asked Mrs Standsfield.

'They seem to get a greater kick out of life than we do. You know how everyone says that teenagers are more honest than they used to be, not going in for hypocrisy and social tact and all that? Well, Jews have always been like that. If we make lots and lots of money we sell the Jag and buy a Mini, though what we'd really like is to buy a couple of Bentleys. But the Jews just buy the Bentleys straight out. And we're jealous and – '

'And think them *nouveau riche?*' suggested Molly icily.

'That's unfair,' said Mr Standsfield. 'I know what our young friend feels – we all did at her age. But as we grow older – '

'We get wiser?' prompted Karen. 'Or too concerned for ourselves to go on fighting for causes?'

'That's just being rather rude.' Molly's tone was prissy.

'I don't think Karen meant anything personal,' I said.

'I meant just this.' She gave me a glance of dismissal as she spoke. 'When people are young and uncorrupted, they believe in causes: they want to fight racialism and the Bomb and poverty. They *know* that right is on their side. Then they have to make a living and come to terms with the old people who control the jobs, and they let themselves be pushed into believing that they weren't right in the first place. But they were. The colour bar *is* wrong; so is the Bomb; *and* letting people starve; and treating Jews as if they were a circus turn.'

There was something magnificent in the way the girl, perched on the edge of her chair, was holding forth, every inch of her passionate with indignation. At that moment I loved her as never before – or after. She was still the Karen who was fun to be with, to go to bed with, have as a steady. But she was also, at that moment, an aspect of a different sort of love. And even as this feeling of love and admiration rose in me, I was aware, too, of the blank hostility of everyone else in the room, particularly of Molly. Karen had spoken out of turn, and vulgarly; she would not easily be forgiven.

'There speaks youth,' said Mr Standsfield at last. 'But you know, dear, it's nothing like as simple as that. You may be right that hundreds of years of persecution have made the Jews what they are – but what they are we don't like.'

'We?' Karen was getting angry now.

I stood up. 'I'm sorry to break things up like this, but Karen and I have arranged to meet some friends.' I looked at Molly. 'You'll forgive us for rushing off.' For a moment I thought that Karen was going to protest that we had no such engagement. I crossed quickly to her chair and held out my hand. As she stood, Molly and then the others did likewise.

I was prepared for Molly to let us see ourselves out, or perhaps ring for the maid. But she followed us into the hall. I wondered whether Karen would apologize and half-hoped that she wouldn't. I need not have worried: with a slight wave and a curt 'Goodnight, Mrs Rapton,' she opened the door and went out to the drive.

I lingered, shook hands and thanked Molly for the drinks.

'Give my love to Julian.'

I nodded. Then, as I followed Karen, Molly called me back. She spoke softly although Karen was already some distance away. 'I don't want to discuss this in any way, David. In any case I think you're old and wise enough to take the point quite simply. Your girl friend is not what I would term suitable material for the sort of work I'm engaged in. Goodnight.'

I mumbled 'I see' and hurried down the drive after Karen.

six

I TOOK Karen home to lunch with me the following Sunday. Nothing was said in advance, but the mere fact of my father's standing influenced our behaviour. I collected Karen from her home, a rare event. She had had her hair done (though with only minimal effect: it was still long and loose and covering almost as much of her face as the back of her head!); and she was wearing a tight, grey woollen dress that made her look sophisticated. And although I was in a suede jacket and sports trousers, I had put on a white shirt and tie. Finally, and again untypically, we arrived on time.

In those days I only read newspapers if I chanced upon someone else's; and watched television even less. Somehow, though, I kept abreast of what was happening to my father and his colleagues, and such ancillary matters as whether their electoral chances were improving or deteriorating. Yet, when Karen's mother said: 'It's getting quite tricky for your father, isn't it, David?' I was lost.

There was a pause, then Karen's father, who was usually content to form part of the background, said: 'He's not been following the news.'

'But surely you talk about it at every meal?'

'Mummy, I told you David's not living at home at the moment.'

In front of her parents Karen always sounded petulant, occasionally childish. Her father was a solicitor's managing clerk. Although it was difficult to imagine him ordering a junior to make tea, Karen assured me that at the office he donned an efficient and almost fierce persona. This was not altogether surprising, since her mother was a dominating personality who sulked obsessively when crossed. At the news of my living away from home, she assumed an expression similar to the one she wore for sulking.

'You haven't quarrelled with your parents?' she asked disapprovingly.

'No,' I answered.

49

While her mother and father waited for my explanation, Karen made a sign that I was not to give it. 'Anyway, what's happened to my father?'

'Sir Brian's had a slight heart attack and is supposed to be giving up, so Corner and Bradley are both after your father to support them. At the same time some of the pundits think he's a dark horse himself.' Karen half-bowed after giving her explanation.

'What a good thing you went to a Grammar School!' I said.

'I thought you were going to David's parents for lunch?' There was accusation in the tone.

'So we are,' answered Karen brightly; and as we had been standing in the hall during the conversation, she stepped to the front door and opened it.

Her father shook hands, then patted me on the shoulder as if to hint at his approval of whatever I did. Her mother half-smiled, but as I was going through the door, asked: 'What's Grammar School got to do with it?'

'Oh, come on!' called Karen, taking me by the hand and pulling the front door to behind her. 'I've told you before, David Coulsdon, you shouldn't tease Mummy. She'll only end up with a sulk and Daddy will suffer.'

'You *are* in a bad mood this morning,' I grumbled. 'That's the last time I traipse all the way out to Ealing to fetch you – and get up in the middle of the night to do it.'

'Sorry,' she answered, suddenly humble; seizing and stopping me, and hugging and kissing as if after a long parting. 'They make me so mad. For the next week I'll have nothing but "why is David living away from home?"'

We went on our way again, arm in arm and enjoying the chilly, autumn morning, the occasional splash of brown leaves on the bare trees and the Sunday morning people: milkmen, car-washers, church-goers and teenagers. Half an hour later we would have been able to add the drinkers to our list, but the pubs were not open yet.

We enjoyed the underground, too, laughing to ourselves at the nearly universal sad, hangdog expressions everyone wore; at the self-consciously clutched bunches of flowers; the sprawling, unmanageable newspapers and the tiny children running up and down the carriage despite their parents' horror. We changed twice and in each train saw, or so it seemed, the same people and the same scenes down to the last yellow chrysanthemum and folded back *News of the World*. And then we walked through Eaton Square as if it was ours, curiously and inconsequentially kings of the morning and pleased with ourselves.

We passed a pub that was open now. Sharp, sexy girls and tall, elegant men mixed with dowdier, county gels and languid, drawling fellahs, union of Chelsea and Belgravia, on the terrace outside. It was cold, but they posed with their glasses, suede jackets and easy cheerfulness as if for a photographer. They were (probably) switched-on or successful or privileged, and they added one or more of these qualifications to their youth. Their Minis and Sprites and Volkswagens stood at the kerb; the Jaguars and Rovers and Humbers belonged to those who were drinking inside. The occasional suburbanite on the way to somewhere else was as out of place as a white man in Harlem.

We arrived on time. My mother came to the door herself and at once made a fuss of Karen. The girl resisted the attempt to rush her upstairs, not even bothering to look in the long, hall mirror, but she accepted the compliments about her dress with obvious pleasure. My mother said nothing about Karen's hair, but I don't think the girl noticed the brief, dismissing glance.

'What are you doing now, Karen?' she asked as she led the way into the drawing-room, a long narrow room that charmed me despite its calculated chic. 'I haven't seen you for ages. When was the last time you were here? Do sit down, won't you? Mark'll be in in a moment: he's just putting the finishing touches to a speech he's got to make to the Society of Incorporated Motor Manufacturers – I think that's who it is – tomorrow night. How are your father and mother?'

'The questions,' I said as dryly as I could, 'may be taken in any order.'

'He doesn't change, does he? Sometimes I wonder how you put up with him for so long.'

'I'm a good lover,' I started because my mother enjoyed being shocked, when father came into the room.

Although he greeted us warmly, his mind was elsewhere. This was confirmed when he put soda instead of tonic in my gin. 'Don't worry,' I said, 'it's the spirit of the thing I'm interested in.' I sat next to Karen on the couch. 'I hear you're a starter in the Highest Office Stakes.'

My father looked mildly shocked. 'Paper talk,' he said contemptuously, 'and from the dregs at that.'

'But, Mark, it could – ' my mother started, then stopped when she saw him frown.

'How?' I demanded. 'Corner and Bradley may stalemate each other but – sorry to be so blunt – there are still two or three others senior to you.'

Mother tried to exchange a despairing look with Karen, but the girl was too interested in my father's reaction to notice.

'You're not quite right, David,' he said after a long pause for effect. 'There are in the party three or possibly four men senior to me in most ways but – ' he nodded his head sagely – 'they are already committed to Bradley or Corner.'

'Won't you have to jump one way or the other?' asked Karen. 'I remember one of our history masters saying that very few political plums had ever been won by sitting on fences.'

'Agreed,' answered my father. 'On the other hand, many are plucked by jumping at the right moment.'

My mother stood up and crossed to the mantelpiece, busying herself with poking the fire although it was burning fiercely. 'Do we have to talk about this?' she asked, her back to us.

'Why not? It's in everyone's mind.'

'Not very much,' said my father quietly. 'I can't pretend to be unaware of the possibility, but if the price is twenty-four hours a day of plotting and scheming, I'd rather wait till next time round.'

I didn't believe this, of course. My father was more ambitious than the next man, and the next and the next. But he hated failure: once he had confessed to wanting to be Prime Minister, he would expose himself to the chance of losing. So I guessed that underneath the patronizing diffidence lay an ache for the position that was as powerful and persistent as Corner's or Bradley's. Knowing this too, my mother did all she could to discourage open discussion.

Looking back, I realize that it was not only the right policy for someone of my father's temperament, but it was a good one at that. Throughout his life he had been underestimated because of this outward show of diffidence and had slid, often unexpectedly, up the ladder. The Communications Ministry was not a senior one; yet I had little doubt that it could provide him with an adequate starting point once he was sure that the other candidates had neutralized each other. For the present he would have to be careful. Communications might be a junior ministry, but it was exceptionally exposed to the public. Millions of motorists would start up in arms at the first false step. The next few weeks – in fact until the succession was settled – would demand cautious treading in every direction.

Over lunch my mother mentioned that she had heard we had been to the Raptons for drinks. 'Do you like them?' I countered.

'I hardly know them, dear. They're very intelligent, I imagine.'

'Karen had a go at them – or rather at some frightful friends of theirs.'

'What about?'

'They were beginning to get rather anti-semitic, and Karen didn't like it.' I looked at the girl for support and she nodded firmly.

'You young people are far too touchy about that sort of thing,' answered my mother in a dismissive tone of voice. 'Who would like a little more beef?'

My father stood up and moved to the carving table as Karen said: 'I don't think so, Mrs Coulsdon. After all, there's no better way of judging a society – or a family or any group for that matter – than by the way it treats a minority inside it.'

'Who'd like some more then?' asked my father. 'Karen? David?' We passed our plates.

'Don't you agree, Mr Coulsdon?'

My father laid the neatly carved slices on our plates with judicious care. 'I agree that in a democracy such as ours we must treat everyone as equally entitled. Another potato? Good. But that doesn't mean that I have to welcome such people socially – or even like them. I wouldn't dream of barring a black from the Savoy, but surely I don't have to invite him here.'

'And what about Jews and homosexuals?' demanded Karen.

My father sat down again. 'The same goes for Jews. Homosexuals are another case: they are outside the law as it stands at present.'

'But the law is *us*.'

'I know, my dear girl, and the Labouchère Amendment remains unamended in its turn because the majority of *us* believe that the community must be protected from homosexuals and homosexuals from each other.'

'And you believe that?' Karen might as well have been arguing with a girl from her old grammar school for all the awe she showed my father.

'Yes, Karen, I do.'

'So you would reject Uncle Julian if he was really in need?'

Both my parents answered at once. 'This is hardly a suitable conversation for a Sunday lunch' (mother); 'I didn't say that at all, David' (father).

As if to emphasize the background against which the conversation was being conducted, my father ponderously helped everyone to more wine. Only my mother refused.

'Look, I don't mean to be rude,' Karen said to her, 'but – ' she turned back to my father – 'wouldn't this country be a better place if we weren't so frightened to discuss this sort of thing? For a Jew, queer or coloured person, his difference is the central factor of his life. He's got all the other problems like earning a living, keeping healthy, voting for a party or making a number of viable relationships, but first on his list is his particular difference. And if he were big enough, we'd regard helping him to adjust himself to us as one of our top priorities.' She picked up her knife and fork with an almost defiant gesture.

My father continued to smile tolerantly, but I sensed that he was becoming angry. I remembered how this had happened about a year ago. I had gone to the House with my mother, arriving in good time to hear him wind up a big debate. Father had listened to reams of Opposition speeches, feet up, smile easily at hand. Then the member for B—— had joined the attack, starting on general lines, but going on to allege that father was protecting a road transport lobby. Suddenly he had swung his feet off the table and jumped up to his own defence. His controlled yet blazing anger had carried his fellow ministers from the first sentence; a paragraph later and the back benchers were cheering his every statement. I remember his taut, superior expression of that night; he wore the same one now.

'Who are these people you're fighting for, Karen? You talk of them as if they were our equals, but they're not. I know, I know: they breathe like us and eat like us and sleep like us. I've also seen the *Merchant* and read fifty books on the subject. But so do animals breathe and eat and sleep. The Jews only look after themselves. Blacks? They'd wipe us off the face of the earth, given the chance. And your precious homosexuals behave with a promiscuity and irresponsibility that no decent man could retail in words. Let all these people start behaving like proper citizens, then talk to me about treating them as equals.'

Karen pushed her plate away. For a moment I wondered whether she was going to leave the table or explode in anger, but she remained silent. She was, though, only finishing a tough morsel of beef. As soon as she had swallowed it, she said: 'If every queer in this country jumped in and out of bed all day and wore lipstick and minced around, and just one behaved normally – normally for him, I mean – then for his sake they must all be treated as tolerantly and sympathetically as possible. I had a history mistress once who used to say that in the social sphere there's a reverse Gresham's Law: people *will* respond to good example and just treatment.' She shook her head. 'Desegregation and legal amendments are only a start. We've very little chance until we welcome all men as friends.'

I had the silly, itching desire to applaud then, for Karen's words carried enough weight for twenty or two hundred people. Yet she could hardly be speaking them more purposefully than to a man who could become Prime Minister before the year was out. I was old enough to know that at that moment he was rejecting them out of hand, but that, planted in his subconscious, they might start eating their way through his prejudices. Perhaps to encourage this I said: 'You know, Dad, you've rather shocked me over this.

I'd always thought you much more liberal, particularly in view of Uncle Julian.'

'Leave Julian out of this!' said my father with a force that made us all uncomfortable.

'Why should we?' I retaliated, clearly aligning myself with Karen. '"One of my best friends is a Jew". "We always stay with an Indian in Calcutta" – but move into the generality and you keep them at arm's length!'

'*David!*' My mother came off the side-lines.

'Uncle Julian's a homosexual, but you entertain him; and his boy friend. And for all his acting and camouflage, Lance Rapton's a Jew.'

Karen gave me a mild, warning glance (I thought at the time that she meant I had gone too far. When we were alone again after lunch, she explained that it was because I had lost track of my argument). It was not enough to stop me, but at that moment the maid came in. Instead of clearing the plates, she turned to my father.

'You're wanted on the telephone, sir,' she said. 'It's the Right Honourable Stephen Corner.'

'Thank you, Enid,' answered my father, adding to the rest of us: 'Please excuse me.'

As the door closed behind him I waited for my mother's little lecture about not making his life more difficult than it was already. And, of course, I was not disappointed.

seven

CORNER'S call to my father, like Bradley's just after tea (we didn't leave until half past five that Sunday) shows how frequently my father's public life impinged on his private. If I omit many of the details, the false trails put out by political correspondents, the series of startling rumours placarded by the evening papers and the half-hearted denials from 10 Downing Street, it is because these are known already. I am not so naïve as to imagine that everyone reading these words will recall the day to day jockeying and bufferings of those few weeks. Even the most dramatic political events quickly fade from all but the participants' minds (there are always *new*, equally dramatic events to replace them: the papers see to that!); but the general sense of flux in this particular race will be vaguely remembered by any newspaper reader of those days. It is only where it directly affected my father, Uncle Julian or me that I am planting an occasional signpost to stir the memory.

I have not said much about myself, though not from modesty. Yet my part in the affair is sufficiently important to warrant more than the gloss I have so far supplied. My reticence stems mainly from the confusion that was so much a part of me at that time. So that, for instance, I enjoyed everything about the Royal College except myself in relation to my work. The students were exciting, stimulating and provocative. They had ideas and ideals, and were not afraid of them. They laughed at convention, accepted ideas and the middle-class thing. Most of them, too, seemed to find some sort of fulfilment in their work, however cynical they pretended to be. Almost alone I felt that my painting was a pretence, a spurious extension of myself rather than a bubbling up of genuine talent.

This dichotomy followed me into my love life. Some of my friends were already deeply and simply in love; others slept around without any desire for permanent union (in or out of marriage). I, on the other hand, was very fond of Karen but concerned to pretend otherwise; and never really knowing whether she was also pretending or loved me as much as I loved her. Any love affair worth the name needs time, energy and endless tactical planning. Ours, at least on my side, required the effort of pretending that it hardly existed. No wonder that when all this was coupled with doubts about my vocation, little time was left for anyone else.

Looking back from the vantage point of a pretty successful art teacher with a wife and two children, I can see that my Scylla and Charybdis of that moment were normal to my age and position. At the time I somehow contrived to blame both situations on my parents: my father for some years had been too preoccupied with his political career to give me the help and guidance I needed, while my mother was similarly involved in his career and her social life. I think we have probably become too conscious of the more obvious Freudian *dicta*: we don't all need the same amount of parental love to flower into whole personalities; nor was I lacking in love *qua* love. But I had never been given advice or guidance in acceptable forms, had blundered on in a mixture of rebellion and bewilderment; and become as inwardly uncertain as I was outwardly confident.

Uncle Julian, almost alone, saw through this. Somewhere else in this tale I think I have mentioned that like most homosexuals he was much younger than his years. Queers who imagine they are still in their early twenties, when in fact they are thirty or forty, are rather pathetic. But the less vain variety retain an ability to talk *with* young people instead of down to them that the normal man may well envy. This was Julian's position in relation to me, but it did not preclude him remaining an 'uncle' at the same time. Although my effective upbringing was post-war, I had somehow absorbed a great number of pre-war middle-class values: after-noon tea, maids with lace-edged aprons, dry sherry before lunch, theatre-going as an 'outing,' meals never to be eaten in the kitchen and so on (to this day I feel uncomfortable in Woolworths, though intellectually I know this to be ridiculous). Many of these values have stuck despite all attempts to shake them off; and with them came the idea that uncles are kindly, elderly advisers.

Had I actually said anything to Julian about my confusion? Or was there enough empathy between us for him to guess? Certainly on my way in that same Sunday night he was able to go almost straight to the point.

'Nice day?'

I nodded. I had intended to go to bed, but he had waylaid me as I came through the hall and persuasively suggested a night cap.

'How's Karen?'

'Fine.' She was, too. I had taken her home, her parents had been out and we had gone to bed together. Not knowing when they might get back, our pleasure had been diluted by the need to keep alert for the sound of their car (Karen claimed she knew its engine from the moment it turned into the road. I conceded this but drew attention to a propeller-to-tail chain of jets that were grazing the roof on the way to London Airport that night). But later, just as one tends to release the brake after gingerly starting down a steep hill, we had let ourselves go; and spent a splendid, carefree couple of hours – and had time to right ourselves and have some food before her parents had returned.

'Is she the only one or just top of the league?'

'Fairly steady.'

'And your work?'

'Not so good.'

'I thought not.'

'Why?'

'Two signposts. Firstly, you're painting lousily.' He held up his hand. 'I wasn't exactly snooping but – how shall I put it, David? – you *are* one of those people who need help in keeping their rooms clean.'

'Point taken.'

'Good. And the canvases I've seen in there bear little relation to the work I remember you doing when you first went to art school. The current stuff is self-conscious and contrived.' He paused. 'Sorry if I'm touching a live nerve.' He pointed at my glass. 'More anaesthetic?'

'No thanks. Second signpost?'

'There are a dozen reasons why a man may be frustrated, but two lead the field: sex and work. I gather sex is pretty well arranged so the trouble must be coming from work. Hold it! – I know what you're going to say. How do I know you're frustrated?'

'Right again, Sherlock!'

'Well, to begin with you're on edge all the time. Too much drumming of the fingers and automatic stroking of the hair for a healthy art student. And you let yourself get defeated, even by little things around the house.'

I raised my glass to him. 'You're good, you know, and right. But where do we go from here?'

'Cures are always harder than diagnoses, whatever the medics may say. Basically you've lost belief in your own talent; and your talent's paying you back by confusing you. Why not try to go back to the time when it all had a genuine ring? See if you can do the same sort of work again without copying yourself, and then let the spirit move you from there. It won't be easy because self-consciousness can't just be shrugged off: it's a major curse for most artists. But it might work, and it's better than building up a first class block, which is what you're doing at the moment.'

I nodded and stayed silent. Any competent teacher ought to have been able to make that diagnosis, but no one had. For Julian, deep in his worries and contradictions, to have put his finger on the sore spot so quickly won my instant admiration. It had a further effect. His very assurance began to undermine my belief in the melodramatic story of his own temptations. No man this calm and understanding could be so seriously led astray in real life. His fantasies were bizarre, to say the least, but fantasies they would remain. And I felt more of the old warmth towards him.

The phone rang. Julian crossed the room to answer, muttering about people who chose to ring at unearthly hours. He gave his number briskly, seemed even more irritated when he knew the identity of the caller, then sharply changed his tone. The conversation was a long one, confined for Julian to 'yes' and 'no' and a few quick questions. I went out to the lavatory, and they were still at it when I returned. 'Shut the door, David, please,' he called, hand on the mouthpiece, then carried on with his monosyllabic comments. At last he finished.

'That was Peter, Peter Dunn,' he said as he helped himself to another drink. 'Remember him?'

'Yes.'

'He and Cy are always asking after you. Want you to go round to their place and all that, but I didn't really think you took to them that night.'

I hope that I looked neutral.

'I don't think I ever told you much about them, did I?' He didn't wait for an answer. 'They run a men's boutique in Chelsea. It's a bit overdone: the stuff they sell, I mean. But they make a good living from it, and it allows them to let their hair down most of the time, as they never tire of telling you.'

I was about to lose interest, may even have missed a few sentences, when Julian said: 'Well this time they seem to have made a right old mess of him.' Peter? Or Cy? I frowned, and Julian started to explain.

It seems that he had known Peter and Cyril for nearly ten years, and that they had been living together for some time when he met them. Since homosexual affairs are usually short-lived, this was something in itself. 'But they're even more unusual,' Julian explained, 'by remaining an affair in every sense of the word.' He peered at me over his glass to make sure that I had taken his meaning. To confirm it I raised my hand in greeting.

With a slight quickening of voice he went on to explain that despite this harmony, Cy had always had his little philanderings on the side. 'For these escapades, he always turns to trade.'

'Trade?'

'Male tarts.'

'Are there?'

'Good God, yes, all over the West End – and elsewhere. And Cy goes to them for a rather curious reason. He says that if he's paying for it, Peter has no need to be jealous since the whole thing's on a cold, physical plane.'

I asked for another drink at that moment, and he told me to help myself. He waited while I replenished my glass, watching me with an odd, slightly quizzical expression. Only when I had sat down again did he add that he thought Cy's reasoning pretty thin self-justification. 'He likes a bit of rough, it's as simple as that. There are plenty of people who'd go to bed with Cy, but not the pseudo-tough layabouts he's looking for.' Julian, perhaps sensing that he was once more losing interest, hurried on. 'He was coming back through the 'Dilly tonight when just such a youth accosted him. Cy showed interest, a price was fixed and off they went to the boy's room in Camden Town.'

I had twice gone with a prostitute, the first time not even real- izing she was one until she brought up the question of money (it was in a bar, I had drunk a great deal and somehow it had been too late to say no when the price was mentioned). The second time I had been sober and went with the girl as a gesture of defiance to a girl friend who had refused to sleep with me, although I knew she slept with other boys. Without the drinks the room had seemed sordid and littered, the girl stale-smelling and not too clean, and the prepayment commercial in the extreme. Yet the girl had had a body that was lithe and soft-skinned and had been expert at her job. So I had enjoyed the act itself despite the mild sense of disgust that had preceded and followed it. I add this not in a sense of bravado, but to show that resorting to prostitutes was not something out of my ken. Yet the idea of that tall, waspish-looking Cy going to bed with (I suppose that is what Julian meant) a roadworker or a van boy was to me almost impossible.

I think my thoughts had made me miss a bit of my uncle's narrative, as when I returned to his voice Cy and the boy were already getting out of the taxi in front of some dilapidated house in the worst part of Camden Town. To show that I was listening, I asked what they talked about on these occasions.

Julian looked surprised by my question. 'God alone knows. From stories of some of Cy's earlier escapades I gather there's a sort of pattern. They exchange first names, Cy asks if the boy works – ' Julian laughed – 'as well, and the boy says "no" but he's got an interview for a job next morning. The talkative ones then ask what Cy does for a living, and he usually says he's a civil servant or a businessman from the north.'

I nodded. We both looked towards the door as we heard some- one enter the house but footsteps on the stairs told us that it was not the actor.

'Canter's late,' said Julian, looking at his watch. 'Where was I?'

'On the front steps of a tumbledown house.'

As the story progressed Julian's telling of it became more excited and confused. I didn't at the time understand a reference to a man and a girl who drew back the ground-floor curtain and peered at them while the boy was looking for his key. Nor did I get the significance of the key not fitting the lock, and the girl (who was about twenty) coming to let them in. In retrospect I gather that they were all involved.

By now I was beginning to find the story a little exciting and was surprised and not very pleased at discovering this. The last thing I wanted to feel was disgust, but it did seem wrong (I nearly used the word unnatural) for me to find the tale even minutely erotic. I began to drum my fingers, stopped when I caught Julian's eye on them, and must have started again: half way through the next lap he copied me then shook his head in disapproval.

It seems that when the boy took Cy into a room at the end of the passage, the girl, who had gone back to the front room, could be heard laughing her head off with her boy friend. If Cy was momentarily worried by them, he was quickly diverted first by the ghastly room, with clothes and tins and dirty washing-up all over the place, then by the boy who immediately started to undress.

Julian's flow was suddenly interrupted, this time for a censored paragraph, I imagined. On the telephone Peter had probably indulged in some physical description that Julian had had to excise before repeating it to someone outside their circle. But he was soon off again. 'They hadn't been in bed five minutes before there was a knock. Cy jumped out and the boy followed. "Don't open that door!" Cy shouted, though whoever it was outside was already threatening to bash it in. Before Cy could pull on his pants, the boy turned the key and three really nasty-looking thugs elbowed their way in. "What's going on in here?" their leader shouted, and when Cy didn't answer, he started to punch him in the face and chest.'

There was a strange intensity in Julian's eyes as he went on with the story, so that I began to wonder whether he was exaggerating. At the same time I was enthralled. His voice was sliding gradually up the scale as he described how two of the thugs attacked Cy while the third went through his pockets. The original one, mean-

while, was dressing and taking as little part in the proceedings as
possible, which led the romantic Cy to believe that he was playing
the stooge against his will. After they had hit him enough, they
told him to get dressed. 'Peter says you wouldn't recognize Cy,
they've made such a mess of him.' And with his shirt tails hanging
out, tie crushed into his pocket and laces undone, he had been
pushed into the street, the couple in the front room still watching
and laughing.

'How did he get home?'

'He staggered to the main road, was lucky enough to get a taxi
and told the driver he'd fallen down some area steps. It was obviously a lie, but the bloke said nothing and drove him home; and
Peter paid the fare.'

We were silent for several minutes. I think Julian was waiting for
me to comment on the story. But I could think of nothing kinder
than a mellow version of 'serve him right!' So I kept quiet. Then,
at last, feeling the tension mounting between us, I asked: 'How
does Peter feel about all this?'

'He's a bit mixed, I think. Cy tries to be discreet about his philanderings, but Peter usually guesses when it happens. He's hurt, of
course, and jealous despite all Cy's reasonings. But he forgives him
in an avuncular sort of way, and they go on till the next time.'

We were silent again. These people lived outside the law, so
there was little they could do when criminally attacked. They
would adduce this too, as a reason for changing the law; and here
Karen would be on their side. But they were wrong, and so was
she. If homosexuals resorted to buying young men, they must
take the consequences. My thoughts at the end of Julian's recital
were neither as clear nor as bald as this, which is informed by after-
thoughts: at the time I was mainly aware of feeling unsympathetic
about the whole business.

I don't know whether my face showed this, for suddenly Julian
said: 'Shocked?'

'Not exactly shocked, but he did rather ask for it, didn't he?'

'David, have you – forget it!'

'Have I what?'

'No, it was a stupid question to ask a good-looking young man.'

The compliment made me feel uncomfortable: somehow it was loaded. 'Have I ever been with a prostitute? Is that it?'

'Yes, it is.'

'The answer's in the affirmative, as my father would say.'

'And if you'd walked into a trap, wouldn't you have been entitled to police protection?'

'That's different,' I answered, irked that he had guessed my train of thought.

Julian sighed. 'It always is. Do you know Britten's *St Nicholas* Cantata?'

'No.'

'It's always been a favourite of mine. Marvellous blend of innocence and boyishness and simple religious feeling. There's an LP of it, conducted by Britten, with Peter Pears and David Hemings as the soloists.' He broke off for a moment as if searching for exactly the words to match the point he was trying to make. 'I don't think you've ever met a friend of mine called Derek Sturton. We were at school together and have kept in touch ever since. We heard this at its first performance at Aldeburgh – I don't remember when: 1948 at a guess; and it became another bond between us.' He ran his knuckles backwards and forwards along his chin. 'Derek's not a queer but he's always known I was, and it's never made any difference.'

I said 'I see', but the story seemed pointless.

'And then one night, after a concert and a lot of drink, I told him what I told you. About small boys, I mean. And absolutely spontaneously – you know, his very first reaction was: "so that's why you're crazy about *St Nicholas*!" "But, Derek," I said, "so are you."'

Julian stood up and looked down at me. '"That's quite different", was his answer, "I'm not queer". We're still in touch, but – ' He shrugged his shoulders. 'We ought to go to bed, David, Canter's going to be very late.' Without a further word he strolled out of the room.

eight

JUST as I have given few details of the struggle for political leadership because they are not central to my story, so I have said little about my life at the Royal College. For this, too, lay mainly outside the particular happenings of that year. Of course, I spent the best part of each day for five days a week at the college, was involved in a number of groups, experiments and relationships; and took part with my fellow students in some extra-mural activities (the one that springs to mind now is the Rag Week). But what happened to Uncle Julian, its effect on me and its even greater effect on my father would have been roughly the same had I been working on a building site or in a stockbroker's office.

If the routine of life drawing, painting, history of art and kindred lectures is not central to my story, one or two of the personal relationships come into a different category. These centre mainly round three people of whom the most important was Rosemary Carlos. She was a dark, quiet girl, already outstanding as a design student, and now, under her married name, a famous dress designer. She was at that time shy and, as a consequence, almost a solitary figure. In the rough and tumble of College life no one seemed to notice her until she began to win lavish praise from the instructors. But some time before this I caught her up one night, hurrying along the Cromwell Road in a sharp shower, unprotected by coat, hat or umbrella. Instinctively I pulled my duffle coat round her and we ran together to the nearest bus shelter.

In the rush and rain of the moment I cannot remember any more whether I held her in a suggestive way nor can I recall whether her closeness aroused me. But the incident removed a barrier on her side and she began to seek me out. Flattered, I spent one or two evenings with her when Karen was otherwise engaged. Finally I found myself, within a fortnight, taking her home and arriving to find the house empty (her parents and younger sister had gone to some relations for the evening). In the middle of some mild necking she surprised me by putting her hand in my crutch. Taken unawares, I knocked it away rather sharply and sat up. The visit was cut short (she had a sudden headache, the twentieth-century form of sulking), and from then on a friend became for a time a mild enemy, and later an indifferent bystander.

Having told this much (and hoping that some chance will bring her to read these words), I ought perhaps to add the missing paragraph. After all, she was a most bedworthy-looking girl even then, and I had no monogamous pact with Karen. But I was certain at the time that the girl wanted a proper affair, was not given to sleeping around and may even have been a virgin. And I was in no position to enter into that sort of relationship with a second girl. I can only hope that Rosemary's pride will, even at this late stage, be somewhat assuaged by these words.

The other two students to impinge on the story I am telling here were Grant Dellon and Martin Bensted. Grant, thin, tall, blond and self-consciously good-looking, came from Boston. His parents hailed from a leading American family, and his rebellion against them and their values had taken him via Paris and Leicester to the College. It could only have been a mild revolt, because they continued to ship him liberal supplies of dollars throughout his six years in Europe. He appeared weak, impressionable and friendly, but these qualities camouflaged a strangely feminine streak of ruthless determination. He also went through friends as easily as others discard paper handkerchiefs.

We met on my first day at College, revealed ourselves as new-comers, and indulged in five minutes' routine daydreaming about how the place would be the liberating force in our lives. After lunch he had crossed the wide bar in The Hoop and Troy to join me; and (so he said) we were 'buddies' (he spoke in those days with hardly any American accent, but his idioms quickly revealed his origin. He started most sentences with 'say' or 'I guess', and held firmly to words like 'sidewalk' even when repeating someone else's story). From that first drink onwards he tended to join me whenever opportunity offered, and sometimes looked a little hurt when I rushed away at the end of the afternoon. Finally, when

Gelber's play about drug addicts, *The Connection*, came to the Duke of York's, he said that he had bought two tickets 'for us'. When I countered that my girl friend might like to see it, he replied that I could always go again. Doubtfully I agreed (Karen's sweet reasonableness often deserted her if she thought she had been taken for granted).

After the show, which he termed 'the real thing' and I thought interesting non-theatre, he took me to a Victoria restaurant called Le Matelot. It was jolly, the food was excellent and the waiters mainly known to him by their first names. It was also way beyond my pocket, but throughout the evening Grant had emphasized that it was all on him. So that when he begged me to come back to his room for a nightcap, I agreed despite feeling very sleepy.

His room was a flat in Pimlico. The house and street were dilapidated Victorian, but his flat was luxurious, though too mannered and affected for my taste. Grant produced balloon glasses and sloshed huge brandies into them. It would be silly to pretend that I saw a warning light when he made reference to my good looks: I had not then lived in the Julian ménage long enough to pick up what now seem such obvious overtones. Instead I became more and more garrulous, via Gelber, about Ionesco, Pinter and Frisch (the last-named was then a fad of mine), until suddenly, and à propos of nothing in my lecture, Grant asked: 'Say, Dave, supposing – I guess this is just a hypothesis – supposing I was to suggest you and I making it in bed together, what would you say to that?'

'I would say "NO", and pretty sharply,' blasting aside in the unambiguous monosyllable all the alcoholic fumes. 'Anyway, I must be off.'

Our parting was awkward, Grant trying vainly to pretend that his hypothesis had been in the interest of art, and myself, hardly listening, unnaturally angry. From that night onwards I had avoided him and, as in the case of Rosemary, greatly underestimated the sediment of hurt pride I had left behind me.

My subsequent dislike, if that is not too strong a word for it, of Grant was one of a number of attitudes I shared with Martin Bensted. In many ways he was the sort of ideal that I postulated for myself in moments of conceited day-dreaming. He was good-looking in a rugged way, tough without being over-muscular and possessed of a personality that projected itself clearly and warmly. We met, curiously, in the Percolator (I was waiting for Karen as usual that evening) and recognized each other from the College. I was surprised, though, to learn that he had been an habitué of the coffee bar for a long time and knew me by sight. It seemed to me that the first time I had ever seen him was in the research drawing class.

When Karen arrived, I introduced them; and they seemed to take to one another well enough. If anything, I was mildly pleased to show off Martin, perhaps (though unconsciously at the time) because I felt that somehow or other some of his glamour rubbed off on me. Karen, too, was very buoyant. Despite her earlier attitude Molly Rapton had telephoned her that morning, they had lunched together and had then gone to a Chelsea hospital. There Karen had been introduced to the Almoner, a brisk efficient-looking woman whose approach had savoured more of a Bond Street advertising agency rather than a hospital. By four o'clock she had been taken on as a temporary clerical assistant in the office.

'Of course,' she bubbled on as she stirred her coffee, 'the pay's almost nothing; though Senior Almoners do get about £1,500 a year.'

'How many centuries does it take to get that high?' asked Martin, adding: 'and stop stirring that damn coffee. The sugar's never done *you* any harm.'

Surprised, she stopped. 'Well, anyway, you can't be appointed till you're twenty-two – as an ordinary almoner I mean – and you've got to get a degree in social studies first, and then you go to a centre for specialized training in medical social work. All of which couldn't be better as I've got two "A" and shoals of "O" levels and Molly says that would easily get me into Birmingham or Durham, both of which give a B.Soc. Sc.' ('Bachelor of Social Studies,' she added for my benefit as Martin took her spoon away) – 'I mean Birmingham does. Durham gives you a B.A. Social Studies.'

'*Gives* you?' I queried to stem the flow.

'Clot, you know what I mean.'

I did, but that was not sufficient to stop her explaining the whole

thing in precisely the detail she had received it from Molly and/or
the Almoner. By then I decided that Martin's interjections to her
story were wittier and more telling than mine, and that it was time
we went to the cinema. I didn't suggest his coming with us, nor did
Karen afterwards raise the point. And Martin himself accepted our
departure equably.

Karen and I usually met two or three times a week, and almost
always on Wednesdays. But three weeks after that encounter at the
Percolator I had to warn her that I couldn't manage the Wednesday.
A South-London department store had offered the College the opportunity of designing and executing some really original window
displays (they were changing their furniture department from Safe
Nondescript to Fashionable Contemporary); and I was one of the
party of four selected to carry out the job. Although we had visited
the store to inspect the windows and had prepared our designs in
detail, we were warned that it would probably take until ten or
eleven in the evening to complete the job.

In the event the windows were ready by half past eight. If
memory serves me well, they were brilliant. If I add that I was in
charge of the party, the adjective may seem very conceited. As I
have already remarked, however, I was almost at a point of despair
about my work and most unlikely to give myself credit unless it
was blatantly due. I was at the time so excited, as we stood on the
pavement gazing at our handiwork and listening to the favourable
comments of passers-by, that I offered the other three drinks. They
were all, though, anxious to get home and refused, so I made my
way to the Percolator; and was thirty yards from it when Karen
emerged arm in arm with Martin. They turned right as they came
out and set off in the opposite direction to the one by which I was
approaching.

The level of our intelligence doesn't seem to matter much on
these occasions: next day we always know what we should have
done. My simplest course would have been to call out to them.
There might have been a few moments' embarrassment, but I
would probably have cured them of each other for always. The
next best step would have been to go to the Percolator as if I had
not seen them, and spend the evening as best as I could. What I

did is inexplicable from this distance, but seemed so obvious at the time: I took a train to Ealing and waited at the bottom of Karen's road until she came along over two hours later. By then I was cold, miserable and wishing that I'd never met her in the first place.

'Whatever are *you* doing here?' she demanded in a startled voice (she looked tired and untidy: they had been necking – or worse!).

The answers came up in quick succession: 'I just missed you at the Perco;' 'how was Martin?'; 'you certainly don't waste any time;' 'and where did the new boy friend take you?' But before any of them could make the grade into speech, Karen took my arm and began to walk me down the road. 'Do you know,' she started, 'the work's getting so fascinating that I don't care two hoots if I don't get into an Art School any more. Take this morning. We've got a kid of twelve in the hospital with meningitis.' We were passing Karen's home now and there were lights on the upper floor, but she looked straight ahead. 'His mum didn't turn up last Thursday or Friday, and when I made some enquiries I found she'd left the district. Luckily I remembered that I'd seen in her papers that his father was in prison. So I rang Brixton and they said: yes, but he'd been discharged last Thursday. I told Miss Walsh and she got on to the prison authorities, and by yesterday afternoon we'd traced them to Brighton. She rang the local probation officer and he promised to try and see them; and just before I came out tonight, he's rung back to say they would have the child back as soon as he was better.'

'Sorry, I don't quite get – '

'Clot, can't you see? They wanted to start a new life in a new place. But they thought the kid was too strong a link with the past and would pull them back. Through my remembering about the father, we were able to trace them, and remind them of their responsibility as parents.'

We had reached the end of the road and instinctively turned right (I say 'instinctively' because the recreation ground lay that way, and I had a feeling that we were going to damn the dangers and inconveniences and drown Martin Bensted in each other). 'But if they don't love the child?'

'Who said they didn't?' Karen was pulling at her hair with her free hand. 'You can't measure love in a bottle, even if people like you think you can. In the moment of personal panic their love for the child took second place. Reminded of it, and shown that it didn't necessarily run counter to their plans for starting again, they were thrilled to reclaim their son.'

We had reached the gateway to the recreation ground (mercifully there were no gates; our reluctance to use the place stemmed from an occasion when we had almost been surprised in the act by a policeman), and I waited for my prophecy to come true. Instead, Karen disengaged her arm and did an about-turn. Her voice changed quality, too. 'David, we have no contract – and you know that. I don't like being trapped or followed or put on the mat. And I won't be, by you or anyone else.' We were back at the end of the road, and she nodded towards the turning opposite. 'You can get to the Tube just as quickly through St Saviour's Road. 'Bye.'

I wavered again, this time between showing my anger, doubling it or pretending indifference. She walked a few paces, stopped and turned. 'And to give you no excuse for a melodramatic night of self-pity – I *did* go to bed with Martin. He's got his own room. See you.'

I echoed 'see you' like a miserable child deprived of all its toys at one sharp blow.

nine

TURNING into the road, Julian's house always seemed like part of an early Passmore painting. It had the same misty softness, trees muffling the edges of the Victorian outlines; the same unfocused masses of colour. At night it had this Passmore quality; by day it was more Carel Weight: strung traceries of branches, cold slabs of pavement and steps. Only in the sunlight was there a hard-edge quality to it: the rectangle of the side wall met by the circle above the front door. I always paused at the end of the road for the pleasure of the picture ahead (sometimes I cut the mental frame close to the walls, at others I took in the side entrance, the house next door, even the foreground side road). But the first night of Karen and Martin I stopped at the corner from sheer fatigue.

I had caught the last train from Ealing back to town, and the last again out to Swiss Cottage. Throughout the noisy, smelly journey I had been buoyed up by my anger. Who the hell did Karen think she was? A bloody, conceited film star or something? She was just a stupid little ex-schoolgirl using up everything in the first five minutes of her adult life. But as station followed station, and the doors chucked and jerked and opened and closed, my anger began to wear thin. I needed Karen right there beside me to keep it on the boil, and she was probably fast asleep in her bed (worse: reliving the experience of the night as she stirred her Ovaltine!)

I staggered on to the house, worn out, too, by over-acting what I felt. For once I wanted a little sympathy from Julian instead of following my usual procedure of trying to slip into my room un-noticed. But it was Canter who greeted me as I opened the living-room door.

'Julian gone to bed?'

The actor shook his head. 'No, he's at the Society of Stock-broking Swindlers' Annual Dinner. Come in.'

Had I known that it was going to be Canter I would have gone straight to bed. Yet now I obeyed readily enough: I was already aware that for some reason it was Canter minus the act. Even when he stood up to pour me a drink, there was less of the swaying-swagger in his walk.

'The show's coming off,' he said as he pressed the soda siphon.

'It's not our night.'

'You, too? Why?'

'The girl friend's found a new area of operations.'

Canter handed me a drink. 'There are plenty of others,' he said quietly, 'if you'll pardon my realism.'

'Same goes for shows.'

'I'd put the odds on your getting another engagement first.'

We drank in silence.

'David, how does your father feel about Julian – and me?'

At any other time I would have ducked the question, but at that moment I was beginning to feel that Canter wasn't such a bore after all. 'The slick answer, I suppose, would be – embarrassed. But it's probably more complicated than that.' I sipped my drink. 'Naturally he'd rather that his brother wasn't a homosexual. In the same way he'd probably rather that, as he is one, he lived alone and kept it quiet. But I think he's sorry for Julian, too. You know, he wants to help him but doesn't know how.'

'I don't think he likes me.'

'He couldn't.' I smiled. 'It's not you whom he dislikes, but whoever Julian lives with. I'm talking as if I'd thought this all out, but I haven't. I'm really only just beginning to understand his attitude myself. So what I'm saying is really a guess, but probably not a bad one for all that. Once Julian set up shop with you, father felt him to be doubly lost. He'd officially moved over to the other camp, so to speak, and would gradually depend more and more on his friends and less and less on the family. Your living together was the symbol for a new life, with new alignments and new allies. Unless I'm imagining it all.'

Canter stared at me approvingly. 'Not at all. Sounds right on the nail to me. But does your father ever say anything about us?'

'In so many words? No. In looks, expressions, tone of voice – yes.'

|

'Disapprovingly?'

I nodded. My father had in fact been rude about the actor on several occasions, though always to my mother and never to me. He thought that Canter was a louche influence on Julian and would eventually bring him into disrepute. All my uncle's queer friends were laid at Canter's door, and the same went for anything untoward in his dress or the décor of his flat. I guessed, too, that Canter would pursue the subject until I came out with the truth, so I changed tack. 'What an awful experience Cy had the other evening.'

'*Awful?*'

'Don't you think so?'

Canter laughed. 'I *don't*. It's precisely what he wants.'

'I don't get you.'

'Cy's a masochist. Deny it as he would to you or me, and probably to himself as well, his aim is to be beaten up within an inch of his life.'

'Oh, come off it!' I protested. I was liking Canter tonight and finding him good company for once, but that Cy should want to be attacked in that way was preposterous.

Canter shrugged his shoulders. 'I can see it's a bit much for you to accept, but believe me that's the situation. In the moment that the pain and humiliation is at its peak, Cy's the sort who suffers a kind of redemption.'

Canter looked and spoke seriously. He clearly meant what he said, but as clearly he had read up some fancy theory and twisted it to fit Cy. After all, Cy didn't go looking for violence in the first place, only sex partners. But I paused at that thought. I was only repeating to myself what Julian had told me, and Julian could hardly be as frank as Canter in view of our uncle-nephew relationship.

'You know, David, I've always had a thing about violence. I saw a lot of it when I was a kid, particularly at school. And I myself was bullied a hell of a lot there, and – '

'Yes?'

'Well, once some kids were teasing and hitting me. I was squalling and miserable, and they'd pushed me down on the pave-

ment. I hadn't been there two minutes – and they were still laying
into me – when I saw my father turn into the road, look at what
was going on – then double right back the way he'd come!'

'No?'

'Yes. So you can see that my interest in violence was an early
one. I've never been much of a reader apart from books on the
theatre – except for books on violence, like *The Black Ship to Hell*.
That took me months to get through – Julian was always teasing
me about it – and I didn't understand it all in the end. But I got
quite a bit of it; and I've read dozens of articles on the subject.
And everything I've read convinces me that it's one of the most
terrifying problems of our time. Not only are there lots of people
loaded with violence, but there are lots of others dying to be the
victims.'

I'd seen *The Balcony* at the Arts; and read *Young Torless* in
Penguins. I knew there had been boys at school who had become
violent or aggressive at the smallest provocation; I had even met a
couple who could be termed sadists (one had beaten a junior black
and blue on his bare bottom, then used a piece of blackmailing
information to ensure his silence). I had also seen the sordid little
shops in Soho with their *History of Flagellation* and kindred titles;
and realized that there must be buyers for them. But the idea that
a man could derive deep sexual pleasure from being beaten up was
more than I could stomach.

'Is Peter also like that?' I asked, more to give myself time to
think than from real curiosity.

Canter laughed. 'Peter? No.'

'But he knows this is Cy's subconscious aim?'

The actor shrugged his shoulders. 'Yes and no. He once told me
that in their early days Cy had had too much to drink at a party.
When they got home, Cy went down on his knees and implored
Peter to beat him. "Whip me, belt me, kick me," he's supposed to
have begged. But – ' Canter sighed – 'when I reminded Pete of it a
year or so later, he denied every word and swore I was mixing him
up with someone else. Of course, I wasn't.'

'Is there much of this sort of thing – in your world?'

'What's the "your world" gimmick, David? Hasn't anyone told

you what goes on in *yours* – tarts dressed up in thigh boots, wives using the strap on their husbands. Julian says that because society rejects us, we're more inbred and have a higher percentage of kinky behaviour. He may be right. But don't let's pretend that the sado-masochistic set-up is exclusive to the gay world, because it isn't.' Canter frowned. 'Now I've forgotten your question. Oh yes, I know: is there much of it? Well – yes and no. Most queers aren't kinky, but there's a fair number who are: leather jackets, boots, whips, SS uniforms, studded belts, trunch – '

'SS uniforms?'

'Yes, sir, from stem to toe.'

Every now and again, at school or college, someone would offer me a piece of alleged pornography: Durrell's *Black Book*, Miller's *Tropics*, Genet's *Thief's Journal*. I'd read twenty or thirty pages, get a couple of mild kicks en route, then get bored and give up. Pornography, not informed by other virtues, quickly becomes dull (I'm not sure that I would any longer dismiss those particular titles so sweepingly). And now this same feeling of boredom and wasted time overwhelmed me. All right, so Canter was a nicer bloke than I had previously reckoned, more honest, more friendly, more intelligent. But what the hell was I doing at twenty past one in the morning discussing the unpleasant details of the kinky world with him? I checked the clock with my watch: twenty past it was.

'Julian's dinner's lasting,' I said suddenly.

'They've probably gone on to a club or someone's flat for a drink.'

'You don't think he's been carried away by a handsome young stockbroker, then?'

'Julian? Good God no!'

'You're very certain?'

Canter nodded. 'You can't live with someone all these years without having a fair idea of that sort of thing, can you? Like all of us Julian has his good and his bad points, but he's very honest. He almost never tells a lie and he's probably incapable of living a double life.'

Even at that age I doubted the logic of Canter's argument. We cast our friends and relations into roles and assume they'll play

them for ever. But they don't. Kind people can become cruel, liars
honest and sad ones jolly. It makes life easier to label people in a
neat, permanent way; but it leads to nasty shocks when they tear
off the labels. At the time I contented myself with saying: 'Then
what makes you play him up?'

Canter seemed unperturbed by the question. 'We've no agreement, you know. This isn't a marriage. He could tell me to go tomorrow, and I'd get no alimony. Of course it would be ideal if we
could satisfy each other in every way; and we did in the early days.
But that doesn't last, does it?'

'I wouldn't know,' I answered neutrally, 'though I'm sure it
won't if you're expecting failure from the word go.'

'I wasn't expecting anything!' The defence came in his first
return to camp indignation that evening. 'For a few years we did
satisfy each other. And I can still satisfy Julian, but he can't do the
same for me. I need other people as well – it's as simple as that.'

I held out my glass and Canter hurried to refill it, finishing his
own drink as he crossed the room. 'As simple?' I repeated, as the
actor stood with his back to me mixing the drinks. 'With Julian
tearing his heart out night after night because you don't come
home.'

Canter swung round. 'I know,' he answered in a quiet, serious
tone. 'What we only do to those we love in the name of need. You
must think I'm number one bastard, and yet – ' he came across
with my drink – 'Julian can't help being possessive and jealous, I
suppose, but that doesn't cool what I feel down here.' He pointed
to his fly-buttons, then went back to his chair. 'You probably think
I never tried, but I did. It would have been hard enough if we'd
lived in the country, miles from gay pubs and gay friends. But just
imagine, I'm on the stage of all things, and we live in a district that
may not be Earls Court or Notting Hill, but still has a tidy queer
population.'

He was talking fluently. This was hell enough, he said, without
any of the more routine variety: H-bombs, starvation and such.
Loneliness was, perhaps, the worst of all, so people needed each
other. Yet once they had formed relationships, their needs were
often incompatible. It might be worse if the sexual, intellectual

or age differences were too pronounced, but for most people just making a life together threw up strains and tensions that made hate as common as love. 'Hell is other people,' Sartre had said somewhere, but that was a half-truth. 'Lack of other people is an even greater hell,' he might have added. So that it was Julian – and – suffering against Julian – and – loneliness that had to be put on the scales.

'But you could make it easier for him, couldn't you?' I nearly added an apology for my intrusion, but caught it in time: Canter was in a mood to accept criticisms.

'Yes, of course. But don't you see? There are so many things he does and says that make *me* see red, and playing him up by going to the clubs is one of the ways I get my own back. It becomes a safety valve for the whole set-up, and without it we'd probably have an almighty row and split up.' He put down his glass and leaned forward. 'This is going to sound a bit corny, David, but you can take it or leave it. Your uncle and I don't really quarrel very much. I know you've heard quite a bit since you've been here, but – ' he smiled to make it clear he was not scoring a point – 'that's mainly because you're here. And I didn't like the way you were foisted on me without so much as a by-your-leave.'

'No?'

'Oh yes you were. I'll tell you the story one day. But what I'm trying to say now is something else. I may hurt Julian every time I go off with someone, and he certainly riles me when he treats me as an appendage. But there's lots that's good in our living together and bits that are bloody marvellous. It's good to know he's here when I get back; to exchange notes after we've met people; to look back on theatres and holidays and films we've experienced together. And there's something else, too, something not so easy to put into words. There are those moments – perhaps once a week or even once a month – when you feel a wave of affection and you catch hold of each other, not sexily or anything like that, but just because the movement expresses what you feel – and that's something that's grown up over the years and is as exciting as a big second-act curtain.'

I found it almost impossible to believe that tomorrow morning

Canter would again be the waspish, camp actor. This surely was the real man, feeling, understanding, warm, sentimental. Yet I knew that he would be; knew it and wondered why there should be such a dichotomy in the personality. It was not enough to tell myself that I was seeing another facet of the same person, for each Canter was so complete as to deny that the other could exist. And I began to wonder whether a different Julian might not have ensured that tonight's Canter would gradually have ousted the other one altogether.

'Were you sent here?' Canter asked after a long pause.

'I'm not with you.'

'To keep a check on Julian so that he doesn't balls things up for your father.'

As soon as he had said it, I knew that I'd always known that it lay behind my parents' agreement to Julian's suggestion. But it had never crossed into my conscious mind until that night. Of course he was right. I could hear my mother saying: 'the great thing, Mark, is that as long as David's with them, they'll be careful not to do anything silly.' Even as Canter waited for my answer, I began to wonder what sort of trouble they had in mind. As far as they were concerned, Julian lived in a settled ménage with Canter, so their only real doubt could be the actor. And how was I supposed to operate as a check to Canter's wilder impulses?

'I hadn't thought of it before, but it makes sense now you've said it.'

'Annoyed?'

'Mmmm. I don't like being used any more than the next person.' It wasn't the whole truth. At that moment I so nearly let the cat out of the bag about Julian's special predilection that I sat there inwardly shaken at the damage I might have done. 'I hadn't thought of it before, but it makes sense now you've said it. It's ironic, too, that Julian is the real danger, not you in your cosy clubs.' I hadn't indeed spoken the second sentence, only been about to, the words were formed but not uttered. But I felt that I had spoken them, checked with Canter's expression to make sure that I hadn't and resolved to go to bed before alcohol and tiredness precipitated a real boner.

'We've come a long way tonight, David. Agreed?'

I nodded.

'Can we go a bit further?'

'I'm getting nervous,' I replied gently.

Canter laughed. 'It's a little agreement I want, not your body –
if that's what you're thinking. You're more Julian's type than mine,
in that sort of way.'

I must have looked embarrassed.

'No,' he went on, 'I mean just this. You ticked me off for hurting
Julian; and you're right.'

'So?' I wished that he would shut up now.

'I want to entertain my friends here while Julian's at work without word going back to him. How about it?'

I hated him then, and none the less intensely for the feeling
being brief. He was putting me in a nasty position; and he cared
very little that his selfishness must turn me into a hypocrite in one
direction or the other. If you talk about morals to most people,
they think of sex. But for every decision about pre-marital inter-
course, adultery or divorce, there are fifty in the ordinary conduct
of every-day life. Julian was my uncle and my host: I owed it to
him to be loyal. But knowing what I did, Canter's intentions were
(comparatively) harmless; and he was appealing to me as a friend.

'What makes you think I'd go running to Julian with bitchy
stories,' I stalled.

'Four out of ten! I want something more positive than that if
you're to get full marks, David.'

Julian's return saved me for the moment. He came in noisily,
slamming the front door and leaving the lounge one open. His
grin was more of a simper, and he was minutely dishevelled. He
had the unfocused look of a Francis Bacon figure, but moronic
rather than sinister. Canter jumped up quickly and swaggered
across to the bottles.

'What are you having?'

'Camp-Harry-and-soda, please.'

We look suitably distressed at his pseudo-pun.

'Fancy finding you two talking at this hour.' He vaguely pointed
at Canter. 'You're usually out, if I'm not mistaken, and you' – he

veered in my direction – 'you usually slide into the house and try to avoid me.'

'Good dinner?' asked Canter, handing him a small glass of Campari.

'What have you two been talking about?'

'You, mainly.' Canter offered me another drink in sign language, then sat down again when I refused (he had already refilled his own glass while pouring Julian's). 'We were wondering if you'd got off with a handsome young stockbroker.'

Julian tensed slightly. 'Don't judge others by yourself!' Canter looked irritated at once, but as he opened his mouth, Julian added: 'I *was* sitting next to a rather pretty boy as it happens.' He turned to me again. 'And what else were you saying about me?'

'The show's coming off at the end of the week,' said Canter quickly. 'And David's girl friend stood him up.'

Julian held out his now empty glass, and Canter got up with exaggerated weariness. 'I always said *la donna è mobile*.' He hummed a few bars falsetto.

'Meaning me?' demanded Canter unexpectedly and with such an edge to his voice that I wondered whether the words had stirred a painful memory.

'If the fez fits . . .'

Canter handed him a larger glass of Campari. 'What's bitten you tonight – apart from the drink? Afraid of my influence on young David? It might be better if you spent more time watching your own leanings and less in worrying about mine.'

I sensed at once that Julian would jump to the conclusion that I had told Canter about his leaning to pederasty, but there was nothing I could do to clarify things. I felt duty-bound, too, not to go to bed, for I was certain there would be one of the worst rows yet when I had gone. Like a dream that can't be shaken off after waking, I could see no way of freeing us from the subject. In their present mood either or both would mock at a new topic.

'And what's our handsome young David been saying now?'

'Nothing.' I answered too quickly, so that it was Canter's turn to look puzzled.

Julian looked somewhat relieved. He leant back and regarded

me through half-closed eyes. 'You know, when you come to think about it, Mark was either very trusting or very naïve to confide you to my care.'

'*Our* care,' corrected Canter. 'And he was neither, just plain selfish. We were talking about that just before you arrived.'

'Selfish?'

'He's scared stiff that you or I will do something sensational that'll blow back in his direction. That's why he sent Romeo here to keep an eye on us.'

Julian sat up. 'Canter, darling, you do talk the most utter balls. Have you completely forgotten that it was I who talked my dear sister-in-law into sending David here as a first step to his getting a place of his own?'

Canter fluttered his eyebrows. 'You know what you can do with that piece of nonsense, honey, don't you? Neither your brother nor his precious wife give a damn for your views about anything – and that's the truth. You're just their kinky brother who's got to be kept in the attic. And if they've got to use their son to help keep the door closed, so what?'

'Thank you,' I said.

'Not to mention, and sorry if it hurts your sensitive little feelings – and my God they are! But Julian has this thing about being an influence here and an adviser there. Look at him – if you can stand the drink-stained sight: *éminence grise* to café society. Yes, and you can smile, David, because I know what you're thinking: my God, listen to that tenth-rate actor who left school before he even learned his twelve times table. But I know a bit of French, and a thing or two in all sorts of departments.'

I jumped up. 'What gives with you two? Julian gets upset if Canter stays out late, so we can presume he cares about him. And less than half an hour ago tells me that Julian's the big thing in his life. But the moment you get in a room together, you start to scratch each others' eyes out. What's the trouble?'

Canter smiled. 'It's probably you, dearie. We both rather fancy you, in different ways.'

'Oh shut up!' Julian lumbered to his feet and walked out of the room, slamming the door noisily behind him. In the quiet of the early hours the sound seemed enormous. In its wake came the realization of other sounds: a car being inexpertly parked; a dog whining pitifully; footsteps on the pavement outside; and something jangling in step with the refrigerator motor in the kitchen. Then came the separated sounds of Julian's shoes being flung to the floor; and I became aware of Canter's heavy breathing.

'Well?' he asked, slouched and exhausted as if he'd taken violent exercise.

'Well what?'

'Our little agreement.'

'Are you still thinking about that?'

'Then what? Or do you think I should be rushing into Julian, kneeling by his bed and begging his forgiveness. Do you know a married couple who are equally happy in bed after ten years? Course you don't! But society, old-fashioned respect for each other and fear of what the other will do if they're found out keeps most people on the rails – and frustrated. And when queers shack up together the same sort of mores apply.' He shut his eyes for a moment, then opened them again. 'But not, David Coulsdon, to me. And since – rightly – I'm not to hurt your uncle, the only answer is your silence.'

'I'm not here most mornings.'

'That's no answer. I'm not going to start fitting my sex life round your working days. Well, come on, which is it to be?'

'You win,' I said quietly.

His energy returned at once. He came over, shook hands and patted me on the shoulder. 'Good lad. Sleep well.'

Canter left the door open behind him, and I could hear them talking. Their voices were low, so I guessed that the actor's victory over me had made him more conciliatory towards Julian. But I was no less angry with myself for having given in. My prime loyalty was to Julian; and this was truer than ever if Canter's surmise about my parents' motives was correct. Encouraging Canter to deceive my uncle was hardly likely to increase the stability of their relationship or lives.

For a few minutes I began to envy the students I had known who still believed in Christianity. They seemed so certain about right and wrong. And even if it was true that when they said 'Christ commanded us to act so,' their reading of what He had said was more important than His words, for them it worked. But unlike them I could not accept innocent children dying, bishops blessing troops going in to kill, churches fighting endlessly with churches. I was left with myself and a vague adherence to the liberal humanist ethic that I had read in Forster and others.

Which brought me sharply back to Karen. The alcohol and the new Canter, Julian's arrival and their argument had temporarily blocked her from my consciousness. Now the pain returned and with it the knowledge that it was a purely selfish pain. She had every right to go out with that handsome bastard from the College, every right to see me or deny me as she wanted. But that wouldn't stop me from showing her that she had made a stupid mistake; and, in the showing, from winning her back. I finished my drink, put out the fights and retired to bed in a transient state of euphoria.

ten

THE room had the soft, fustian quality of a Sickert. Everything was brown. The girl stood by the window, only just discernible although it was light outside. At first I thought it was Karen, then I realised it was the tart I had once picked up. She was wearing a bra and panties and was staring fixedly at the door. It seemed to take me an age to swivel my head to follow her gaze, and when at last I managed it, there in a still deeper gloom was Martin and not-Martin. He was dressed in jeans, a donkey coat and long, pointed shoes. He had Martin's features, but they had become so coarsened that he looked dangerous and threatening, rather than debonair. Momentarily I was puzzled by the Francis Bacon reproduction hanging by the door, for it was one of the paintings that I hadn't transferred to Swiss Cottage. Then I realized: I was back home in Belgravia.

The thought seemed to make me dizzy, and I wondered whether I had had too much to drink. I glanced at the girl and saw that she was beckoning to me. As I started to move towards her, the figure by the door began to glide towards me; and in a huge, echoing voice, reminiscent of our life instructor, she asked me what I was doing. When I said nothing, he warned me that unless I kept away from the girl and paid him £30 by nightfall, he would expose my father to the newspapers.

For a long moment the scene went hazy, then I was standing by the window next to the girl, gently stroking her bare arm. It was cold to the touch like the arm of a marble statue, but I was still conscious of the deep sensual pleasure of the act. Behind me the thug was beginning to threaten more violently, though I could no longer decipher the exact words; while outside on the road that led to Belgrave Square I began to see two policemen. When they started to look at the house, I waved to them with my free hand. Failing to catch their attention, I began to move my arm more wildly, and redoubled my efforts when they were joined by a reporter whom I had always found friendly. But all three continued to see nothing.

Suddenly the door opened and a shaft of light lit the room.

'What's going on here?' my mother's voice demanded. It was so aggressive that I was terrified that the thug would strike her (and, in a different sense, I was equally terrified that she would understand why the girl was there).

'David! *David!* Come on!'

The voice had changed from my mother's to Julian's. I sat up, conscious of the dishevelled bedclothes, the prickling of cold sweat on my upper lip and the loud beating of my heart; and somehow still enveloped in the ethos of the other room.

'Yes?'

'It's your father. On the phone.'

'What time is it?'

'Ten to eight. Hurry up! Sounds as though he's in a mood as it is.'

I crawled out of bed, noticing for the first time that Julian was half dressed, dark trousers showing from under his dressing gown. He smelt of after-shave lotion, talc and toothpaste, violently hygienic to my senses still caught in the dirty dream. As I made for the lounge, he caught my shoulder and steered me towards his bedroom.

Canter was in bed, asleep or pretending to be. The room smelt stale and was only just lit by a two inch opening in the curtains. For a moment I felt myself drift back to the aura of my nightmare, then I shook myself physically and picked up the phone. Julian, meanwhile, ostentatiously busied himself with selecting a tie from the wardrobe.

'Yes?' I said.

'Good morning, David. How are you?'

'Tired. And you?'

There was a pause, probably to indicate disapproval. I could almost smell that my father had bathed and shaved, and read *all* the daily papers.

'Have you seen this morning's – ' Julian banged the wardrobe door, but I just caught the newspaper's name.

'I certainly haven't! Your call woke me – via Julian.'

'Have you been giving interviews to reporters?'

'What do you think?'

'David, I'm not being funny. There's a half page smear article describing the goings-on of a smart set that has a lot of implications I don't like. And you're right in the middle of it, coming out of some disreputable club.'

Canter was not bothering to pretend sleep any longer: he had even lifted his other ear off the pillow, no doubt in the hope of catching some of my father's words. Julian, meanwhile, was picking at an invisible stain on the tie he had chosen.

'I hope you realize that this couldn't have happened at a worse moment. As you must have read or heard, I have decided to stand for the leadership to avert a major division in the party; and nothing could do me greater harm than this sort of gossip.'

I finally came out of my dream. 'Look,' I said, perhaps more aggressively than I had intended, '(a) I didn't know you were chasing after the Premiership, (b) I have never given an interview to anybody, (c) I haven't even seen the paper. And (d) you of all people should know what these papers will invent to make a story, particularly if they don't like you – and I mean you, not me.'

Canter opened his eyes and winked. I winked back, then glared at Julian who was going through the same slow-motion process with cuff-links as he had with ties.

'David, I think you'd better come to see me before you go off to College. How long will it take you to get here?'

'About an hour.'

'You can take a taxi – at my expense.'

'Fifty minutes then.' The prospect remained disagreeable. 'Can't I come to your office around coffee time? I can do without the College till after lunch' (and for the rest of the day if there was going to be a lot of gossip).

'I've an important committee meeting. David, this business is very serious. I don't make many demands on your time but I'm determined to get to the bottom of this. I shall expect you here by nine.'

I reluctantly agreed and hung up.

'Which paper?' asked Canter, while Julian made a rather ineffectual keep-out-of-this head-shake.

I told him.

'I've always told Julian we're too narrow just having the *Telegraph* and the *Financial Times*.' He turned to my uncle. 'Can we have a pop paper from now on?'

Julian remained on his dignity. 'I don't censor what you buy or read. Is Mark really upset, David?'

'Seems to be.'

'What does it say?' asked Canter sitting up.

'Minister's son goes wild at queer party.' I was nearly at the door.

'NO?' shouted Canter hopefully.

'No,' I answered regretfully.

From the taxi, half an hour later, the red buses had the luminosity of an Allen Jones painting. They were like huge toys, with cheerful negro conductors clinging to their open platforms and dismal white men waiting to jump off them. Almost everyone looked irritated, car drivers particularly. Happy to delay my arrival for as long as possible, I enjoyed it all; even the fare would be met by my father.

Once or twice I thought of stopping the cab to buy the paper, but I preferred my reactions to be spontaneous. Then, during a long hold up at the Orchard Street crossroad, I wondered whether to phone Karen. She would already be at her office as she started at half past eight; and I could suggest lunch, a wild expensive lunch at a Chelsea bistro (on money 'borrowed' from my mother). Once, I could have been certain of my reception. Now I guessed that it might pay to think twice.

My mother greeted me in the hall with an 'Oh David!' to which 'Oh Mummy!' seemed the only answer.

'It's high time you grew up and stopped being a burden to your father – especially at a time like this – ' we said together.

I felt, at that moment, a sudden, irrepressible sense of joy, an instant relief from – from – but that I couldn't place. This upset my mother (not unreasonably): in the face of my father's ambitions, I ought to have glowered like the people on the buses. Besides, she could sense that my uplift was secret, and it was my secrets above all that she resented. 'He never keeps anything from me,' she would tell her friends, always failing to convince herself or them. And she particularly hated the little whispered conferences and laughter that were so much part of my relationship with Karen.

My father was waiting, posed, at his desk.

'Hullo. Eight bob including one and six tip,' I started.

He frowned ominously.

'The taxi. You said you'd fork up for it.'

'David, for the last time will you please realize that this isn't a joke?'

'And will you please stop treating me like a naughty child?' I sat down. 'Does it never occur to you to trust me? Or that the last thing I'd do is give an interview to anybody?'

'At a time of crisis you can't expect me to hold an impartial enquiry into everything that goes wrong. I have to operate on the broadest of fronts.'

'Oh come off it, Dad, *really!* Saving the party, averting a split and all that *dreck*. You want to be Prime Minister? That's perfectly reasonable, for God's sake, so why hide behind all this other stuff when you're talking to me?'

My father recoiled as sharply as if I'd thrown a glass of cold water in his face. 'I just don't understand this heartless cynicism that you young people keep parading.'

'Cynicism? Truth, you mean. Whenever we rip off another piece of hypocrisy, you old people yell "cynic"! But what's the good of pretending to me you give a fuck for the – '

'David!'

'And that bit of shock is as phoney as the other. You know the word, you used it ad nauseam in the war and you know as well as I do that it just fits what I was saying. So why pretend to be outraged? And why treat me as a bloody criminal because everyone within five miles of you is newsworthy?'

My mother somewhat spoilt my speech by coming into the room at that moment. 'David, have you had any breakfast?'

I shook my head.

'Would you like a boiled egg?'

'Two please, and not as hard as concrete.'

'What *is* the matter with you this morning?' she demanded.

'Nothing,' I said. 'You're both a bundle of nerves and as prickly as hell.'

My mother swept out of the room, her expression of distaste twisting to pain as she scraped her hand on the door latch. My father gave her a sympathetic glance, sighed deeply, then handed me the paper. It was folded so that the article on *The Gay Young Things* was uppermost. In the centre of it was a revolting photo of Karen and me coming out of the Percolator. I remembered at once when it had been taken. A few weeks ago we had been to a party given by one of Karen's girl-friends, a spindly excitable creature who enthused volubly about the last novel she had read, the last play she had seen, and so on. She was the daughter of a rich Jewish watch manufacturer (it was from him I had learnt the word *dreck* that was probably still puzzling my father); and they were generous parents. So there had been a great deal to drink and we had emerged tipsy. It was then that I had suggested the Percolator so that Karen wouldn't seem too high when she got home.

At the coffee bar we had had two espressos apiece, but it had done little to sober us. When I had started cupping my hands round Karen's breasts and loudly challenging anyone to measure them, the owner had quietly suggested our leaving. Unfortunately we had turned our exit into an exhibition, cavorting, dancing and necking our way on to the pavement. I remembered now that there had been a flash at the time, but I had probably thought it a prank by some other drunkard (if I was really conscious of it). The paper I had in front of me showed that it had been in earnest.

My father waited patiently while I read the article. It was a masterpiece of innuendo and *double-entendre*. At one level it was a harmless account of mild goings on among the well-heeled in Chelsea. At another, where people read between instead of along the lines, it spoke of sexual promiscuity, alcoholism, homosexuality, drug addiction and general corruption. And there were Karen and I at the centre of the whole thing! Worse, there were just enough facts about my life at the College, with my uncle and at the Percolator to suggest an inside informant. Surely Martin wouldn't . . .

'May I ring Karen?'

'Yes.'

She was brusque but not unfriendly: the Almoner had just arrived and would be wanting her within the next few minutes, so there was no time for gossip. I explained that I was with my father who was very upset by an article in this morning's paper. We spoke quickly, back on the old wavelength. Yes, she had seen it. Yes, she was put out by it. Yes, it could be Martin.

I put my hand over the phone. 'Will you stand us a lunch?'

My father shrugged his shoulders, then said 'yes.'

'Can you manage lunch, pet?'

'Yes, as long as it's a fairly quick one.'

Within a minute we had arranged it and rung off.

'Who's Martin?'

'A mutual friend.'

'Can you get hold of him?'

I stood up. 'Look, Dad, aren't you making a mountain out of a molehill? Whatever damage is going to be done, has been done already. They're not serializing my goings-on, are they?'

My father sighed wearily, and for a moment I was sorry for him. He looked whacked before the day had properly started. 'David, you may laugh and champ at the bit, but you're still an infant in this game. Once this sort of paper gets its teeth into you, it doesn't let up. So see if you can find out if this Martin or someone like him is doing the feeding. Our only chance is to put a stop to it straightaway.' He paused. 'How's Julian?'

'Fine.'

'Settled?'

'Dad, just what do you want to know?'

My father sighed again. 'Go and eat your breakfast. The next week or two is bound to be tricky and I can't pretend it doesn't make its mark.' He stood up and gazed out of the window, the faraway look in his eyes somehow cultivated and yet still true to the moment. 'I'm sorry if I chased you over this, but when the odds are against you from the start, you need every trick in the pack.' He turned away from the window and tapped the paper which lay on the arm of my chair. 'That's why I didn't like this. And why I'm nervous about Julian.'

'*And* why you sent me to live there?'

That broke the mood. He sat down at his desk, alert, posed, the Minister again. 'We suggested your going to Julian because it seemed the ideal compromise between your wishes and your mother's fears. I'm pleased it's working out.'

My mother looked in. 'Your breakfast's ready.'

'Coming, dear.' I moved to follow her. 'Tell me,' I said, 'could a Julian-Canter scandal spoil your chances?'

'Possibly – though probably not. If the smear by association could be made to stick in this sort of paper' – he tapped it again – 'there are quite a few members who'd withdraw their support, I suppose.'

'I'll do what I can,' I said, 'but it would be safer to send them to the South of France for a month. It's legal there, or so they keep telling me.'

My father swung back to his papers with a slightly petulant air; and I was satisfied: I had no intention of leaving him with the feeling that he had won all along the line. 'Don't forget the eight bob,' I said to his back as I went to leave the room, 'and lunch for two at a decent restaurant. You gave me your word for both.' I sounded flippant but inside I felt slightly afraid: not even the South of France would permit Julian's particular peccadillo.

My mother made sure that I had everything I needed, then left the breakfast room. She had probably decided that I was in a sufficiently unpredictable mood to make everyday chit-chat dangerous; or perhaps she wanted a quick consultation with my father. But my feeling of well-being persisted, its champagne edge hardly dented by my father's heavy-handed act. As I started on the eggs I began to question its origin. It had come on before I had phoned Karen, so it could hardly be ascribed to the promise contained in our little exchange. It certainly had nothing to do with being woken early, or finding Canter more amenable than I had anticipated (and Julian strangely unamiable). But nothing else, surely, had happened. Nothing – except that my father was in the running to become Her Majesty's Prime Minister!

I think moods go in cycles, and the cycles themselves are acti-
vated more by the subconscious than by everyday events. The
prospect of an exam can be depressing, but it's possible to wake
with the identical feeling any morning. You feel down because
you feel down; you feel good because you feel good: at least at
the conscious level. Yet even those of us most sympathetic to the
idea of the irrational in our natures continue to look for reasons
for our daily states. So I settled for the fact that I was bouncy
because of my father's success, overriding the voices reminding
me that I thought public figures worthy of pity rather than
envy, the pursuit of power, a disease rather than a virtue and
my father's particular fustian outlook more likely to hinder than
further the country's interests. Mentally I pinned a huge 'I like
Mark' badge on my leather jacket; and emerged from the breakfast room in so generous and conciliatory a manner that both my
parents must have thought me guilty of some as yet unknown
crime.

I spent the morning at the Tate, then met Karen at five past
one. The Librarian at my first Art School, a painter *manqué*, had a
theory that restaurant lighting was inversely proportional to the
charges: in the dearest you could hardly see the food. Certainly the
one I had chosen for this lunch promised to be expensive: although
there was bright sunshine outside, the little basement tables had
to be lit by candles. I had, however, chosen it for a purpose. Karen
and I had eaten there the first time we had been out alone together
(early meetings at the Percolator were never alone in any sense);
and I wanted to strike a nostalgic note. Neither my father's good
news nor the unexpected attack in the paper had more than temporarily pushed Martin Bensted below the surface. Unexpectedly she
brought his name up even before we had time to order.

'I phoned Martin at coffee time – what a business it is to get hold
of anyone at the College even when you say it's important.'

I nodded admiringly: I could never remember a student being
brought out of a class to answer the phone.

'He'd seen the photo, too, and was just as furious as us. Of
course, as soon as he said what a mean trick it was, I knew it
couldn't have been him.'

I wanted to ask whether that was simple trust or feminine logic, but the waiter came for the order. I can never understand why dusters are considered more suitable than aprons for people who serve in these darkened cellars, but that's what he was wearing over his jeans. If it was meant to look exotic, it was only coy; if it was meant to emphasize classlessness, it was merely repetitive: the waiters were all Italians anyway. Ours had little English, but this didn't stop Karen turning her choice of dishes into a long and amusing exchange while I wondered why Martin should be 'furious' at the photo.

'But,' she said to me at last as she handed the poster-sized menu back to the dark, good-looking waiter, 'he thinks he knows who it was.'

'I'm not with you.'

'Martin, you clot! Don't you remember what we were talking about?'

I nodded.

'Well, anyway, he thinks it's an American called Dellon. Martin happened to meet him one night in a Chelsea pub, and Dellon was with some newspaper gossip writer. When this chap left him, he thanked Dellon for the information.'

'Hardly conclusive,' I said, knowing that she was right.

'No, but something Dellon said after the chap had gone leads Martin to think that you'd been one of the things they discussed.' She began to break her roll messily, crumbs splintering all over the table. 'Do you know this Dellon bloke?'

'I do.'

'Like him?'

'He loathes me.'

'Why?'

'Wanted me to go to bed with him and I refused a bit sharply.'

'You always seem to be getting mixed up with those sort of people.'

'That's an accusation.'

'Well you are.'

'Perhaps it's because I'm so good-looking.' When Karen made a small rude noise, I added: 'You want me to prove how queer I am, then?' I checked that the level of lighting was really low, then slid my hand under the table.

'David Coulsdon, you're a very sexy, badly controlled young man!' For a moment she looked at me tenderly, then as she removed my hand from her thigh, she said: 'You can prove it at the first convenient opportunity.'

'This afternoon?'

'Now don't be a clot! *I* work – and you ought to.'

The waiter brought Karen's avocado and my vichyssoise. She immediately preferred my choice to her own – until I offered to change.

'No, I chose it, I'll eat it.'

'What martyrdom!'

'What are we going to do about Dellon?'

'What can we do?'

'Frighten him off, I should think. Warn him that we know he was responsible and will make things difficult if he does it again.'

'Hold it, pet! How? He hasn't done anything illegal – nor, unfortunately, has the paper. That's the trouble with this slimy, smear journalism. You can't pin it down.'

'We can still frighten him – or, rather, I think Martin could.'

Which placed me squarely on the horns of the proverbial dilemma. I wanted to help my father by foreclosing on further gossip items, but I didn't want to owe Martin Bensted anything. It was enough that I had to compete with him without Karen being able to remind me from time to time that I ought to be grateful to him as well.

'Why Martin?'

'He's the sort these Dellons are usually afraid of.'

'And I'm not?'

She looked at me quizzically. 'My God, David, my going to bed with Martin has hurt your pride, hasn't it? You didn't used to be like this. What's happening to you? All of a sudden you're as possessive and jealous as a Victorian housewife.'

'Sorry,' I said, putting my hand on hers. 'I suppose I'm much fonder of you than I've always pretended.'

'And I am of you,' she answered promptly, making it impossible for me to continue the argument. A few moments later she scraped the bottom of her pear for the third time and explained that Martin, as an outsider, might influence Dellon. As an interested party I would have much less chance. Grudgingly I agreed.

'Anyway,' Karen continued, 'aren't you terribly excited about your father becoming PM?'

'He's not there yet by a long chalk. Besides, I thought you couldn't stand Tories at any price.'

'I can't usually, but this is your father. Besides, he's rather cleverer than most of them, isn't he?'

'That's difficult for me to answer.' And it was. Even that morning I had read two profiles of him that seemed absurdly eulogistic. But then it was only natural since I had little or no evidence of him as an administrator or committee chairman, two qualities in which he was supposed to excel. He was also a skilful operator, a good parliamentary speaker and a reasonably hard worker. I am sorry in a way to sound so lukewarm, though this may be inevitable in the face of our relationship. Certainly I was also proud of him. He was already only one step from the top and had reached that height entirely by his own efforts. If the particular ladder hardly seemed worth the climb, I still realized that to most people it was a considerable achievement. Because some of us cannot see the point of climbing Everest, we don't necessarily underrate the feat of doing it.

'Molly seemed terribly excited at the idea that he might get the job.'

'Molly?'

'Oh, of course, I didn't tell you. I saw her yesterday. And I think I know why she started by washing her hands of me, then doing an about-face and getting me the job.'

I raised my eyebrows in query.

'I think she wants me to influence you to persuade Julian that his actor friend ought to go off on his own.'

I looked incredulous.

'Well, she told me that he was having a bad influence on Julian; and if only she knew someone who would give Julian friendly advice, she'd approach him. After a pause while I said nothing, she asked if I thought you'd help.'

'The bloody cheek!' I leant back to let the waiter take my plate. 'What did you say?'

'That I'd talk to you.'

I banged the table so hard that several people sitting nearby in the gloom looked round. 'My God, all you women are just the same. But you'd better read, mark, learn and inwardly digest this, Miss Karen: I am not repeat not interfering in my uncle's private life.'

Karen was unimpressed by my raised voice and table banging. 'I wonder,' she answered mysteriously. And turned her full attention to the steaming plate of *pollo marengo* which the waiter put in front of her.

eleven

HINDSIGHT allows me to admit that some of my show of disinterest in my father's political fate was affectation. Perhaps the best proof of this is that once I started to read the newspapers and watch the box, I became an addict. Probably dating from the very day of my lunch with Karen, I turned from morning papers to evening papers, waded through the highbrow weeklies and watched every programme that touched on the struggle. Nor had I realized how much of each newspaper is devoted to sheer conjecture! By the day of Molly Rapton's cocktail party, the odds were fractionally against my father; but he was still in the running. (Two days later, as some of my readers may recall, he had reversed those odds. His unexpectedly brilliant appearance on television had a profound effect on public opinion and, more important, on Tory MP's as a whole. If his skilful lobbying of individuals continued to meet with equal success, he might yet make it.)

In my Royal College days I still believed that dramatic events started, exploded and ended dramatically. Now I've learnt that often their roots are casual and their endings not much more than a whimper. For the newspapers it all started that night at the hotel in Stratford-upon-Avon. The true beginning was much less direct: it was Lance Rapton's departure for America.

I was surprised to receive a formal invitation to the party. 'What's this in aid of?' I asked Julian at breakfast, pushing an immaculately printed card across the kitchen table to him.

'Lance is off to the States this week. They usually give a party before he goes.' Julian helped himself to more toast. 'Molly rang me the other day and said she wanted to ask you: did I think you'd come?'

'Why me?'

'Because your mother and father are being invited.'

'I don't get that. Is she asking Karen?'

Julian shook his head. 'No, I'm afraid your girl-friend – is she still that? Oh good! – I'm afraid she put up a black last time she went there.'

'Then why did Molly take the trouble to get her the job?'

Julian finished his coffee.

'You?'

He nodded. 'When you told me about your fiasco of a visit, I had a word with Molly. As soon as she saw that I wanted her to help, the status quo ante-party was restored.'

'*Thank you*,' I said with a slight bow.

'It's all in the day's work, saying which – I must be off. You'll come to the party?'

'You want me to.'

Julian nodded his head vigorously.

'Then I will.'

'Good man.'

I had assumed that Canter would be going, but when the evening arrived, it was just Julian and myself. Weakly, my uncle explained that Molly must have thought that Canter was still in a show (what excuse Julian had made to Canter I couldn't imagine: he certainly would not have accepted that one). In any case it was not really Canter's sort of party.

'Nor mine, I imagine.'

'Not exactly, but you're the son of the guest of honour.'

I was not happy about this particular, nor about formal cock-tail parties in general. This had always been true, but currently I was growing my hair longer than was acceptable in the square world; and at that moment I did not want to compromise my father. Parents tend to get over-heated about this question of hairstyles. Karen had once shown me a book by a psychiatrist named Charles Berg who had a hep theory about it. The punch line, which is all I remember, is that to a parent the hair of a male child is tied up with his virility. Cutting off his hair equals cutting off his sexual maturity, equals keeping him dependent for longer. Or something like that. So quite apart from the aesthetic effect, I was symbolically inclined to let it grow. But Molly's formal, elderly guests would hardly know about such subtle psychological twists; and I was hoping that they wouldn't include a bunch of MP's.

They did; and a fair number of other celebrities and near-celebrities. Waiting to be greeted by her, I wondered whether my father had been used as the main magnet; or whether his name had merely helped with the first few who were then dangled before the remainder. Watching Molly exchanging welcoming words with a best-selling novelist and his pinch-faced wife, I became certain that the Raptons had decided to promote my father. They – or perhaps it was only Molly – had probably made up their minds that if they could help him to power, they would at least be able to establish a salon of influence where politicians and creative artists could meet. Or perhaps they had greater ambitions than that. Julian, to whom I suggested all this afterwards, thought I was nuts. Certainly when Molly caught sight of him she dropped the novelist and his wife and hurried forward.

The long drawing-room was already fairly full and the buzz of conversation rose steadily. Disconnected words seemed to reach me from all over the room, but I could hardly hear what Molly and Julian were saying to each other. White-coated waiters with trays of champagne moved anxiously between the crowd; and a maid patiently offered a silver dish of canapés. I recognized no one, not even the leading 'pop' artist to whom Molly introduced us when the pressure of new arrivals in the hall demanded her attention. The artist (he must already be forgotten: in those days he was a name in art circles but I have seen no mention of him now for quite five years) looked bored at the prospect of talking to a student from the College. Then there was a stir at the door: my mother and father had arrived.

'Jeese,' said the painter in pseudo-American, 'there's that gob they keep propping up on video.'

'Our future Prime Minister, perhaps,' I answered, checking first to see who was standing near us.

'If he makes it, I'm for the gas oven. Isn't there anything else we can do in this country except shove clocks back? How's about us forgetting Victoria for a while?' Tall already, he edged up on his toes. 'Jeese, there's that pansy brother of his talking to him.'

Now I was shaken. Already feeling a little guilty for not having defended my father, I felt worse at not refuting the description of Julian. But I was even more concerned at how he had come by this opinion. Was this generally known? In what circles? Was it already doing my father harm in drawing-rooms like this one, where arts and politics mingled briefly? 'What makes you think he's like that?'

The painter lowered himself and looked at me pityingly. 'What for would he live with that crap actor otherwise? Unless you're supposing it's to cover his heterosexual traces?' His expression changed. 'You a friend of his?'

'We're related.'

'Don't tell me he produced a son as well?'

'I'm his nephew.'

He turned from me to where Molly was introducing some important-looking people to my parents. 'I'd stay clear of him if I was you. Stick to friends, eh?' He smiled then started to move away.

I found the encounter bizarre and disturbing. I couldn't think why he disliked Julian so much (my father was another matter: young painters are apt to despise Tory ministers). I began to wonder whether my uncle had dozens of enemies, though that seemed unlikely. He was rarely envious or malicious, or even successful to a degree that might antagonize others. He was, too, friendly, gregarious and helpful. Even at this moment I could see him talking and laughing with a small group of people for all the world as though this type of gathering was his natural habitat.

'Hello, young man!' I turned quickly: it was Mr Standsfield. 'And how are you?'

'Very well, thanks.'

'So am I. No girl-friend tonight?'

'No.'

'That's a shame,' he said with a smile. 'I rather took to her. You don't often meet young people with that sort of spirit these days.'

'I'm not sure Mrs Rapton felt like that,' I ventured, checking that Molly was still near the door.

He leant towards me and lowered his voice. 'I think that was because your young friend touched on a sore spot.'

'Really?' I tried to sound innocent.

He came still closer. 'The Raptons are Jewish, I'm told.'

'Are – or were?'

'There's no past tense if you're born that way, young man. Once an ikey, always an ikey.'

Mr Standsfield's glass was empty; and from his leering, slightly fuddled manner I guessed that he had had two or three drinks already. He stood up to one side of me, his lips still close to my ear, and I followed his look to where his wife was talking to the best-selling novelist. Beyond them Lance could be seen with my father and mother, and in the hall Molly was again with Julian.

'That's not all,' said Mr Standsfield. I could feel his breath on the side of my face. 'They say she's very keen on that uncle of yours.' He laughed vulgarly. Mercifully someone made a sign to him and he waved back, allowing me to dart away before he could say another word.

So that, too, was a subject for gossip: Molly's feelings for Julian. But how was that reconciled with the other rumours? Or did the two stories spring from different groups, the heterosexual from the smart, Belgravia crowd, the homosexual from the bohemian circle? None of it could do my father much good, yet at this moment he looked completely unaware: smiling, talking, seeming confident and exuding an air of goodwill to all who were introduced to him.

Lance left England two days later; and within twenty-four hours of that Molly began to show her hand more openly. It would be an exaggeration to say that she threw herself at Julian. For one thing there was a core of dignity in her character that restrained her; for another Julian started by giving her encouragement. Even as we had said goodnight to the Raptons towards the end of that party, Julian had said to Lance: 'And don't worry: we'll look after Molly.' Lance had seemed delighted, so Julian added: 'What about a theatre next week, then?' The way was open for her to telephone; and she had seized the opportunity joyfully.

At first it was mainly the telephone, although I was aware that they had twice been out together. Then she started to call, sometimes just for a drink, sometimes for a meal. Once I came back to find her there alone, arranging some flowers (had Julian given her a key, then?). Canter was barely polite to her, while she made little effort to win his approval. For the first fortnight after Lance's departure Julian seemed delighted with her attentions. Then, suddenly, I felt his attitude change.

I don't think I was fully alive to the change for a few days: it's only in retrospect that I realize I had noted it subconsciously. On the surface all seemed to be going well until the day Julian said: 'If that's Molly, say I'm out,' leaving me to answer the phone. For the next few days he even seemed to stay out more than usual. Molly reacted predictably by phoning and calling more than ever. She even invited them to dinner when Canter, at home by himself, answered the phone. He told Julian this as soon as we arrived (my uncle and I had met coming out of the Underground).

'Oh God, I do wish that woman would leave me alone for a bit.'

'Don't look at me,' Canter replied. 'She's your friend, not mine. Anyway, she's expecting us on Wednesday.'

As they talked on, I began to wonder what had led to Julian's sudden change of attitude to her. Had she, perhaps, made some sexual overture that had shocked him? This hardly fitted with Molly's outward character, but sharper contradictions were not uncommon. After all, the whole situation was odd. She knew that Julian was queer, and that he had a satisfactory homosexual relationship with another man. Or had Julian innocently misled her by running down Canter? Even then, it was difficult to believe that she could see herself as the actor's successor.

'I've never understood why these women make a bee-line for queers,' said Julian unfolding his evening paper.

'Frightened of real men,' suggested Canter. He was pasting press-cuttings into a huge green album.

'What's that supposed to mean?'

'What it says.' He glanced at me. 'Even David can understand that. If a woman's subconsciously afraid of sex, she'll fall for a queer, knowing she's safe.'

'Where did you learn that one?'

Canter put down the paste brush and turned to me. 'See? If he says something clever, it comes from having a brilliant brain. If *I*

say something, it's where did I learn it? I may not have your educa-
tion, Julian Coulsdon, but I've got a bloody sight better brain than
you in some directions.' He stopped as the phone started to ring.

'If it's Molly, I'm not in yet,' said Julian.

'Has she been groping you or something?' asked Canter, standing up with an effort and crossing to the telephone. 'Hullo?' There
was a pause. 'It's for you, David.'

It was Karen. Molly had been in touch with her to know whether
we would come to dinner the following Wednesday. I told her to
hold on, put my hand on the phone and repeated the invitation to
the others. 'Do you want us to come?' I asked.

'I shall be away,' said Julian after a moment's hesitation.

'Where are you going?' demanded Canter.

I was never to know if Julian's plans were already in existence
or were a reaction to my question. Free will or Fate: could he
have changed his mind and agreed to come after all? Or was it all
decreed in advance, if not by God then by some Pattern of Living?

'To Stratford,' said Julian evenly. 'It's quiet at the office at the
moment, so I thought I'd take a few days off next week before the
season there finishes.'

'Sorry to keep you waiting,' I said into the phone at last. 'Julian's
going away next week.' She interrupted to ask what that had to do
with it, and I explained that they had also been invited for the same
evening.

'For crying out loud,' said Karen, irritated now, 'do you want to
go or not?'

I didn't want to at all. The more I saw of Molly Rapton, the less I
liked her. But now she was an ally of sorts for my father; and, more
important, it would give Karen and me an extra evening together.
Recently she had been seeing Martin and me, her time arrogantly
divided between us. Somehow a dinner at Molly's seemed to assert
my priority. 'OK, OK,' I said, 'let's go.'

Looking back over the years and being mainly concerned to tell
the story of my father and my uncle, I may have given the impression that my concern about Martin Bensted was quick, strong and
transient. At the time I was profoundly disturbed by it for weeks
on end. I resented everything about it, but chiefly their having sex

together. In despairing moments I would visualize them together, feel him running his hands over her taut, smooth body, feel him covering and entering her, entwining his legs with hers, finding his excitement and security inside her. I tortured myself with this and tortured myself with the obverse that he had as much right to it as I had. In any case I was afraid to protest too much. Karen was intelligent, but she was also immature and wilful: she might cut me off altogether to teach me a lesson. And that would have been much worse.

Actually, on the Sunday before Molly's dinner her parents went away for the day; and we seized the opportunity to spend the afternoon in bed together. It was wonderful – how, with Karen, could it be otherwise? Yet it was somewhere below peak. Was this because she was no longer committing as much of herself to our coming together as before? Or because I kept thinking: this is where he was last Tuesday or Thursday or whenever they had last met? Once I could have discussed this with her. Now I was afraid she would bristle ('if it's not good enough for you, why don't we drop it?'). As it was, there was no obvious tension, and we spent the evening listening to Thelonious Monk.

At one point, as I went to turn over a record, she asked: 'What was all that about your uncle on the phone the other night?'

I ran an Emitex round the unplayed side. 'Oh that. Molly's got a thing about Julian and has been chasing him like mad ever since Lance went to America. He seemed to like it at first, but about a week ago he did an about-face. Doesn't even want to speak to her on the phone any more.' I put the disc gently on the turntable and lifted the arm. 'When he heard about the dinner party, he decided to buzz off to Stratford.'

'What's he going to do there?'

I sat down beside Karen again and took hold of her hand. 'Shakespeare, pet. Ever heard of him?'

For answer she kissed me lightly on the lips.

twelve

KAREN and I were the first to arrive for Molly's dinner. During the Monday and Tuesday I wondered whether she would make an excuse to cancel it when she knew that Julian wouldn't be coming. He had sent her a note, according to Canter, polite, friendly and alleging that his trip could not be postponed. From the same source I understood that the visit was now planned to last most of the week: on Friday Lance was due back. But we heard nothing from our hostess; and when she greeted us in the hall, she was charming and vibrant. She was also smarter than I had ever seen her, which is saying something.

As soon as we were seated in the drawing-room she disposed of the subject of Julian. 'Your uncle's very naughty, David,' she said. 'He could easily have interrupted his business and come to town tonight, and gone back tomorrow morning. As it is, I hope you'll be able to tell him what a good dinner party he missed.' She turned to Karen. 'And how are you getting on, dear?'

Karen launched into an account of her day-to-day activities. She described the people she worked with, and what she was learning; and added, as the bell rang for the next arrivals, that she was becoming so absorbed in the work that she had given up all idea of becoming an art student. From the start I was jealous of the animation she was showing, but her final piece of news, of which I had had no advance indication, really put me out. Fancy telling Molly about it before anyone else!

'You serious?' I said urgently as Molly left the room.

'I certainly am.' She pulled at her long hair ineffectually. 'Martin's furious.'

'So what?' jostled with 'Then *I'm* delighted', but I just nodded. Molly came back a moment later, leading a young couple into the room. The girl had deep, mournful eyes but an otherwise eager expression; the man had long hair and wore a tight, waisted flannel suit (musician or painter?).

They were introduced as Alan and Fiona Duncan; we were left as plain 'Karen' and 'David'. I offered to pour the drinks and Molly, nodding in reply, set the conversation going, explaining that the Duncans were musicians. And although they had two fairly small children they both managed to teach and to play in public. While pouring the drinks I watched them carefully and noted that there was something odd about them. My attempt to define it was cut short by Canter's arrival. Molly let the maid bring him into the room instead of going out to greet him in the hall as she had with the rest of us.

Although they permitted themselves to be introduced formally, I sensed that Alan Duncan and Canter knew each other already. The meeting, too, served as a catalyst to my puzzle: Alan was even more feminine than Canter; Fiona was quite masculine. This is not as unusual as is alleged: most of us know men and women whose dominant traits are more often associated with the other sex. But Alan Duncan's femininity was particularly wistful and unprotected. Returning to my seat, I began to wonder whether living with Julian was beginning to make me hyper-sensitive to such situations.

The remaining guests were a couple in their early thirties, the husband being in advertising; and Desmond Avery, a brilliant rising lawyer. The conversation quickly settled into two groups and, as far as I could hear, centred on the theatre in both cases. Alan Duncan, in my circle, was a persuasive adherent of the 'new' theatre, and his face lit up as he spoke of Beckett and Ionesco. I began to warm to him and noticed Karen sharing my reaction.

When dinner was announced, Molly shepherded us to the dining-room (a comparatively small but beautiful room, ornately furnished in good taste); and I found myself bringing up the rear with Canter.

'The Duncans are rather fun,' I said softly.

'He's queer as a corkscrew,' answered the actor.

'But they've got kids!'

Karen, just ahead of us with Desmond Avery, turned to frown at us for speaking too loudly.

'So what?'

But we were in the dining-room where I found myself sitting on

Molly's right. The Duncans were further down the table, but twice I found him staring at me in an odd way. Or did I think it 'odd' because of what Canter had said? While I answered Molly's questions and occasionally took part in the talk at our end of the table, I began to toy with a new thought. If Canter was right, had the Duncans been invited to show Julian what was possible? But now I was running off the rails. Whatever Molly's feelings for Julian, no one had suggested that she was unhappy with Lance; or considered leaving him.

The dinner was good. I looked after the wine, the maid served, and Molly, in the role of conductor, led and controlled the conversation. She seemed determined to show the sweeter side of her nature, and was successful enough for me to begin to question my earlier opinion of her.

Towards the end of the meal there was a lull at both ends of the table.

'Have you got a new part yet?' she asked Canter.

However endemic 'resting' may be to the acting profession, Canter clearly hated the question. 'As a matter of fact I'm considering several offers at the moment.'

'What are they?' she pressed, while everyone else watched the actor.

'Don't tell them!' put in Karen quickly. 'It's bad luck to do so.' Canter, blushing now, gave her a grateful look.

'That's a very new superstition, isn't it?' asked Molly smiling.

'Well, at least tell us what sort of offers.' Fiona Duncan's voice was strained. 'I didn't even know you were an actor, so I'm quite in the dark.'

Canter, speechless, was crumbling. I jumped in with the name of his last revue, adding: 'Surely you saw that?'

'We only go for straight things,' explained Alan Duncan, with hardly more than a suspicion of intellectual arrogance.

'It was a pretty good show on the whole,' said Karen, 'and Canter was damn good.'

Molly pushed back her chair. 'Shall we retire for coffee?' she asked, then, standing, addressed herself to Canter. 'I'm terribly sorry but I never saw it either. Every time I wanted to go, Julian forbade it.' She laughed as she pushed back her chair. 'I shan't let him dissuade me from your next one though.' Taking Alan Duncan's arm, she led the way to the drawing-room.

As the maid brought round a silver tray with cups of coffee, sugar bowl and cream jug, I found myself with Desmond Avery. Karen was beside me on a small sofa under the window and Canter, really nearer the group round the fireplace, was trying to appear part of ours.

'Are you related to the Minister of Communications?' asked Avery. He sat in an upright armchair in the corner of the room, a little tense, but also a little puzzled.

'He's my father.'

'Lucky I asked that question first.' He smiled in a friendly way, but without losing his air of alertness.

'What would you have said, then?'

He paused as if waiting on the spin of a coin for the right answer. 'That I hope he won't make it.'

'In this drawing-room?' I asked, showing by my tone that I bore him no resentment for the remark.

'Why?' demanded Karen before he could answer.

'Oh mainly because he might just save the Tories, and I don't want them saved.'

There was silence, then Canter asked: 'What sort of cases do you defend?'

'And prosecute?'

But Canter missed Avery's meaning. 'I mean, do you specialize?'

'Not really.'

'You'd take any case?'

Avery appeared to consider Karen's question at length. 'No,' he answered at last, 'I don't think I would. All things being equal, the right fee can persuade me; outside that I'd rather believe in what I'm doing.'

'Are you married?' asked Canter.

'No.'

'Would you defend someone accused of a homosexual offence?' (He glanced down the drawing-room as he spoke).

'Are those two questions meant to be related?' The lawyer was smiling now, and relaxed. When Canter blushed, he added: 'Because that isn't why I'm not married, if that's what you were getting at.'

'No, of course I wasn't – I mean . . .' Canter was hopelessly embarrassed.

'Would you take such a case?' Karen pressed.

'But of course, not least because it covers one of the bad patches in our law.'

'What does?' asked Molly, crossing to us, and suggesting that Avery should join the advertising agent and his wife before anyone could answer.

For the rest of the evening the conversation remained safe: foreign holidays, West End restaurants, Sunday papers and the difficulty of getting Covent Garden tickets took up most of the time. Only once was the even tenor of middle-class chatter disturbed. The advertising agent told how he had been kept waiting for two hours at a hospital despite being the specialist's private patient. 'Who do these specialists think they are that we've always got to be at their beck and call?' Avery counter-attacked at once, brusquely ruling privilege out of court in a modern world. Following on quickly, Molly moved the conversation, via Karen, to almoners, and the argument was still-born. But it made it even stranger that she should have included a left-wing lawyer among her guests.

As soon as I felt that we had stayed the accepted span of time, I asked Molly to excuse us, explaining that I had to take Karen all the way to Ealing and then get back to Hampstead. Canter left with us. On the way to the Tube I asked him if he had met Alan Duncan before.

'I'll say! We picked each other up at the Gay Sailors Club one night, then found we were both at the same end of the pole.' He looked at Karen, probably to see if he had shocked her. 'And I bet Molly only invited that Avery because Julian once said how much he admired him.' He stopped at the crossroads. 'Look, I'm not coming home yet. I said I'd look in at the Club if we got away early. O.K.?'

'You do as you like.'

'See you then'; and he was gone.

Karen and I walked on towards the Underground. 'I don't like that man,' she said firmly. 'He's got a one track mind and I'm not taken with the particular track.'

'That's intolerant, for you.'

'I don't mean it like that, and you know it.'

'Look!' I said.

'What?'

'There's a cab. We could be back at Julian's in quarter of an hour and your last train isn't till 12.40, and you don't mind going home alone, you always say so.'

Karen laughed. 'And you're on the same track as that pansy, even if you do go the other way.' But when I started to call 'Taxi! Taxi!' she joined in.

It felt strange letting her into the flat when neither of its owners was there. She must have felt this, too, because she became skittish and over-excited, running from room to room with short, jumping steps. When I tried to keep her in my bedroom, she insisted on using Julian's. Finally we landed up on the drawing-room sofa, pulled askew to face the electric fire.

As we lay there in the growing warmth, our haste fell away. We became drowsy and carefree, forgetting time and place; and aware-ness of last trains and Canter's return was gently edged out of conscious reach. Ever warmer and more comfortable, our imme-diate world was gradually filled with the knowledge of each other; of our young, exciting bodies; and the love that flowed through that physical contact. So that when the phone rang it came as a cold, violent shock.

'Oh God!'

'Let it ring,' said Karen, eyes closed, hands caressing my shoul-ders and back.

But after a few moments I began to sit up. 'It may be Julian,' I explained, though really I was thinking of the people in the base-ment and on the first floor, both of whom must have heard us come in. I lowered my feet to the floor, Karen watching me through half-opened eyes.

'You do look funny,' she said.

'No funnier than anyone else in this state,' I retorted as I reached for my shirt.

'You don't have to dress to answer the phone, silly.'

I threw the shirt at her and went to the phone, noticing that the clock showed that we had missed the last train. The voice at the other end was gruff and strange, and I had difficulty in focusing the words. Besides, it took time to explain that I was not Canter. Then that I was Julian's nephew. And finally (how weak!) that there must surely be some sort of mistake: my uncle could never be in *that* sort of trouble. Then I promised that Canter would phone as soon as he arrived, took the number and put down the phone.

Dazed, I went back to Karen. We stayed there, half lying, half sitting for another ten minutes or so. She asked no questions, but I guessed that she had understood all from my few remarks to the police sergeant. Details, after all, are superfluous in such a situation. This was vaguely confirmed when the brittle, aggressive tenderness of her lovemaking gave way to a more protective softness. Each stroke of her fingers told me that she was there supporting me.

'We must get a cab, darling,' I said at last. I stroked her hair. 'Do you have any money?'

She looked at the clock now. 'Oh Lord! The damn train's gone.' She sighed. 'It's going to need an awful lot to bribe one to take me as far as Ealing.'

I nodded and disengaged myself. Without a further word being spoken, our mood changed. We dressed quickly, straightened the couch and turned off the fire. I scribbled a note to Canter to wait up for me and left it on his bed. Then Karen and I set off briskly to Swiss Cottage, holding each other tightly, guessing that the same urgent, frightening questions were beginning to attack us simultaneously.

It took us nearly twenty minutes to find a taxi-driver who would make the journey westwards. Only then, as she was about to get in, did Karen ask: 'Is it – well, very serious?'

'I'm afraid so.'

'Keep in touch, won't you?'

'Of course.'

She climbed in, gave the driver her address and lowered the window. 'It would happen just when I was beginning to get fond of you. I was only – ' But the driver was in no mood for delay. With a throaty roar the taxi drew away; and as she went, I felt for the first time the full impact of Julian's news.

thirteen

ILLOGICALLY I strolled. I knew that the return phone call to Stratford was a matter of urgency and that Canter might soon be home. I am not sure, even at this distance of time, why I went the longest way back to Julian's flat. Of course I wanted to put off the moment of telling Canter and all that would follow from that. But I delayed for some less logical motive; perhaps a need to commune with the night air before committing myself to the inevitable crisis.

So I walked towards Haverstock Hill, re-living not so much the time between the dinner and the phone call as that between the call and our finding a taxi. There had been a tenderness in Karen whose depth I had never touched before. As I ambled and watched, watched the late people scurrying home and the stray cats and the bare, expressive mass of trees, I began to wonder whether we could perhaps make it together. At that age I didn't know that tenderness and consideration for the other person were the two essential ingredients in any close relationship; I only sensed it. But as I finally set my footsteps in the direction of the flat, the blight returned. How did I know for sure that she wasn't showing the same tenderness to Martin?

Canter was in the lounge waiting for me. He had fallen asleep over the pages of a magazine, but woke when I came in. He looked sleepy and hostile: perhaps he thought I was going to pick an argument over the abrupt way he had left us. In any case it meant that he had been in for some time and was waiting for an explanation of my absence. Instead I launched into a recital of the phone call from Stratford and the brief details given me. And his instant concern saved me from having to invent an excuse to cover my delayed return.

'What do I say to them?' He was shaken and unsure.

'I don't know. Perhaps they need someone to vouch for him.'

'Wouldn't it be best to phone your father?'

It would and it wouldn't. Julian would probably be released if my father telephoned the police station. But if that one call reached the ears of the press, the end of all father's ambitions might be in sight. Equally, the end of Julian's career might ensue from failing to offer every help. I expressed all this to Canter.

'No,' he said quickly, 'it's not like that. Not even your father can rescue Julian if he's already been charged.'

He was fidgety yet calm, his fingers nervously picking at the loose covers, his responses more logical than mine. He explained briefly that several of his friends had been in trouble from time to time: the lesson learnt was to play everything down. In this case, too, Stratford was miles from London. Only Julian's surname gave the thing an extra, potentially enormous danger. 'But why a boy?' he asked twice, in a tone that made it sound as if Julian's choice had been a personal affront.

'He likes boys.'

'Who? Julian? Never!'

'That's what he told me.'

Canter's look of hostility returned. He got up and began to pace the room, then stopped to pour himself a drink. 'What do I say when I get through?' he asked plaintively. 'Can't you get your father's advice on that?'

I nodded doubtfully. Somehow it seemed imperative to keep my father out of it altogether. It was not only that he might get his fingers scorched by helping; it was also that he wouldn't understand a word of what he was told. *Indecently assaulting a thirteen year old boy.* What on earth could this have to do with his middle-class, stockbroking brother, Julian?

The thought of Julian's name acted as a trigger: for the first time that night I began to think of him. So far we had only thought of the act and its consequences. What about the victim – or, rather, the victim we knew: the boy was only a concept. What was Julian thinking and feeling at this moment? Wasn't he already suffering for all the harm his action would entail for others? He would be sitting (or lying?) in some dingy prison cell, turning over and over the outcome of what he had done. *Indecent assault.* What did it mean? And to my horror I found myself wondering whether at least he had succeeded before being caught. Or had the child simply yelled as soon as Julian had moved to touch him?

'Look,' said Canter, suddenly, as if he had come to a decision. 'Whatever happens, you must ring your old man. For one thing he may save us from dropping an awful brick. For another he's bound to be involved. . . .' He paused, searching for words.

'. . . if only in keeping uninvolved?' I suggested.

'Yes. Come on!' He moved towards me. 'Please. I just can't be without Julian – not for long, I mean.'

I dialled my father's number, hoping that he would answer himself. As the phone started to ring I wondered at Canter's reaction. Didn't he care, then, about Julian's unfaithfulness? (Strange word in the circumstances, but what other would do?). Or would that concern come later, after he had been reassured that Julian was not to be taken from him? The phone stopped ringing, there was a pause and then my father's sleepy voice. 'Yes?'

'It's David, Dad. Sorry about this but Julian's in a spot of bother and I'd like your advice.'

'Yes?' He sounded alert and wary now.

'Can I come over?'

'How?'

'Taxi.'

'Right.'

For a moment I thought he was going to say that he was coming to us; in fact I nearly suggested it. Then I realized that it would attract far less attention if I let myself into his house at three in the morning. I explained this to Canter who, to my surprise, insisted on accompanying me. I countered that it would be more discreet if I went alone.

'Why? There won't be a crowd of reporters at this time of night, will there?' He came towards me again. 'Besides, I don't want to be left alone.'

At this distance the mixture of stability and instability, calm and panic, still puzzles me; at the time I was simply irritated. With a grudging 'OK' I motioned him to follow me, certain that my father would find his presence unwelcome. Canter hurriedly put on his jacket and coat, then we left the house. There were no taxis to be found, but a motorist in an off-white Austin stopped for us in the Finchley Road. He was going to Victoria and would drop us in Grosvenor Gardens.

'Miss the last bus?' he asked as we settled in the car, me in front, Canter in the back.

I laughed guiltily (could *he* be a reporter?). 'No. Stayed too long at a party.'

He drove in silence for a few minutes then: 'Good party?'

'Fairly.' Do shut up, I thought, shut up, stop asking questions and get us there as quickly as these stupid red lights will let you. I guessed that my father was already grey with anxiety.

As soon as we got out of the car I started to run, but Canter rightly held me back. 'You'll have the coppers after you if you start running at this hour of the night,' he shouted in a whispered tone as he tried to catch me up. 'Look,' he said, drawing level, 'you'll have to do all the talking. Your father scares me stiff at the best of times. OK?'

'OK,' I agreed.

My father must have seen us coming, for the door opened as we approached the house (warming to the sight of him, I didn't even notice whether there were any policemen in the shadows, though I am sure there were no reporters). He had put on his trousers, socks and slippers and over them wore a heavy silk dressing-gown. It had a dark Chinese pattern, huge tassels on the belt and looked very opulent. Watching it swirl as he hurried forward, we followed him into his study. If Canter's presence irked him, he gave no sign of it. We had both been briefly, wordlessly shaken by the hand when he let us in.

Unusually he sat on an upright chair away from the desk, while we shared the tiny sofa adjoining the bookshelves. 'What's happened?' he asked as soon as we were seated.

'We don't know very much,' I answered quickly, 'except that the Stratford police rang to say Julian had been charged with the indecent assault of a thirteen year old boy; and would Canter ring as soon as he got in.'

My father turned to Canter. 'What happened then?' he asked impassively.

Canter looked at me. 'That's why we came to you,' I explained. 'This only happened an hour or so ago and we were both late in. And we didn't want to say the wrong thing.'

What did my father feel at that moment? Despair? Disgust? Nothing showed. All his planning and struggles of the last few weeks were suddenly threatened by something that must have seemed utterly repulsive to him. Yet when he spoke, his voice was soft and measured. 'I think the best thing you can do, David, is to take your mother's car and drive straight to Stratford. When you arrive at the Station, send our friend here in to see Julian.' He paused. 'I'll come down to Hampstead just before lunch. I won't be able to stop long, as I want to be at the House at two: I'm winding up on the Traffic Act later in the afternoon. But I'll bring Roy Gater, my solicitor, with me.' He stood up. 'Hold on a moment and I'll get the keys of the Morris.' He left the room.

'But supposing they won't let Julian go?' said Canter. 'I don't think your father understands the position.'

'He understands it better than you think – certainly the legal side and probably the other, too.'

We were silent for a while then Canter, glancing round the room, said: 'It's a fabulous house, isn't it?'

I grunted noncommittally as my father came back. He handed me some keys. 'Your mother says would you like her to get up and make you some eggs and bacon before you start?'

'No, thanks.'

My father looked at Canter, who shook his head and mumbled: 'No, thank you, sir. Could I use the toilet though?'

We went into the hall and father pointed to a door at the end of the corridor. 'I'll come out to the garage with you in case the constable on duty wants to know what's going on,' he said as the actor waddled away. 'Don't phone me from Stratford unless you have to and don't allow yourself to be interviewed by anyone. Even the words "no comment" can be dangerous in this sort of situation. Not that anyone is likely to question you. Coulsdon's not a very common name but that shouldn't have led to anyone tying up Julian and me as long as he's kept his head. Right?'

I smiled and nodded agreement, then we were silent for a

moment. 'By the way,' my father went on in the same even tone, 'if you both came back late, as you put it, who took the original message from the Stratford police?'

I heard the chain being pulled, the water flushing and the door of the lavatory opening. 'I did – but I'll explain that later,' I said quickly, jerking my head towards the end of the corridor from which Canter appeared at that moment.

My father led the way through the front door which he left open. A policeman on the edge of the pavement turned, narrowed his eyes, then smiled and saluted. Having acknowledged his greeting, father unlocked the garage and slid back the wide, rolling door, making hardly any noise in either operation. I shook hands with him, then jumped into the Morris. For a moment I thought it was going to give trouble, then the engine fired. I shot into the road, paused long enough to let Canter get in, then streaked away towards Hyde Park Corner. In the mirror I could see my father chatting to the policeman.

From Hyde Park Corner to Western Avenue Canter and I quarrelled. Over and over again he wanted to know why I had not asked for more explicit instructions from my father. Each time I answered that it was sufficient to do as he told us: if you go to people better informed than yourself for advice, you should trust them and follow it. As we passed along two sides of Shepherd's Bush, he varied the questions by asking how I could take the whole thing so lightly; after all, it was my uncle who might be sent to prison, my father whose career might be marred.

'*Lightly!*' I exploded as we turned sharp left just beyond White City. 'For Christ's sake, Canter, if you can't say anything more sensible than that, button up. You're like a pregnant whore who can't make up her mind whether to have it or drown it.'

Shocked or offended the actor said not another word, and we drove for the next hour in silence. As the sense of travelling and drawing away from London began to envelop me, the events of the last few hours assumed a dream-like quality. Had there been a phone call from Stratford at all? Or was the whole thing, this thinking about it as well, a folly of a nightmare? Although I knew that I was awake, that the Morris was draughty and its steering wobbly, I could not completely shake off the sense of unreality that cocooned everything since Molly's dinner party. It was as if the recording part of my brain was out of alignment with the rest of my senses.

Approaching Woodstock, Canter, plaintive again, asked: 'Look, would you mind going into the police station for me?'

'You heard what my father said.'

He sulked then until Shipston, gazing fixedly out of the side window. Then – 'When did Julian tell you he liked little boys?'

'Some weeks ago, while you were on one of your late jaunts.'

'Don't bitch.'

We were silent until Newbold, a faint premonition of dawn light giving an Ivon Hitchens look to the intervening countryside, gnarled, twisting, elemental in form. The car sounded hot and rattly. We had hardly driven above sixty (probably what the motor correspondents call 'a genuine fifty-five'), but the fussing and buzzing of the little machine magnified the speed and exacerbated our tiredness.

'He's never even looked at anyone below eighteen.'

'Purposefully, perhaps.'

'Meaning?'

'He was ashamed of it.'

'He didn't have to be. You can't help how you're made, can you? Not that I like them young, 'cause I don't! But why not tell me of all people?'

We were approaching Stratford. 'Perhaps because it's in front of you of all people that he wants to maintain a certain image of himself.' I slowed again for a signpost. 'And an image that you of all people have been responsible for creating.'

'Why do you hate me so much, David?'

'Oh shut up, you stupid baby! Hate. Love. You people throw words around as if they weighed nothing at all. I'm tired, I'm fed up and I can see my father about to lose the one thing he's really wanted in all his miserable life – and all you can say is: "why do you hate me so much?" If you really want to know, I don't give a fuck for you; and I certainly don't think you're interesting or important enough to hate.'

After that, silence was absolute. Except for the night when we had been alone together in the flat, Canter had always seemed like a spoilt child to me. His present behaviour confirmed it: he was completely immature, a straight case of arrested development. Even Julian's precarious position meant nothing more than the risk that he, Canter, might be deprived of his adopted 'father'.

We motored about Stratford for ten minutes before seeing a constable whom we could ask the way to the Police Station. He looked at us suspiciously, then slowly explained our route while his eyes examined the back seat of the car and the floor in front of it. Thanking him briefly, we set off. A hundred yards from the building, as soon as we had caught sight of the blue lamp, I swung the car into a side road and stopped. 'OK. Off you go – and all the best.'

Canter was in pieces now, stuttering and trembling, the colour (as far as I could see) gone from his face. Twice his dimly perceived look asked 'Must I?'; twice I nodded back towards the main street. At length he pulled himself out of the car, gave me a weak, sloppy wave and ambled up the road. As I watched him disappear I wondered whether he would actually enter the Police Station; or come back after five minutes crying that he couldn't pick up the necessary courage. But when ten minutes, then quarter of an hour, had gone, I guessed that he had somehow managed it. And was relieved.

Are we conscious of the watersheds in our lives; or do we attach the labels with the help of hindsight? The results, of course, are the same. From the moment of leaving school to the moment of seeing Canter disappear was Part I; from his return to my leaving the College at the end of three years was Part II. However dimly I perceived the significance of the moment when I saw him (in the mirror) coming back round the corner of the road, I was aware that there had been a modulation in the tenor of our lives. Nothing would ever be the same again, proclaims the cliché; and the cliché, as so often, is right. Nor was I deceived by the actor's quicker, lighter step that all was necessarily well.

He opened the door, stopped, threw himself in and uncoiled in the seat. He was slightly breathless. 'We ought to have phoned first,' he started. 'What Julian needs is money and there was enough in the flat. He always keeps some hidden there for emergencies.'

'*Touché.*'

'What's that?' But he was not going to wait for an explanation. 'The police'll let him out on bail if we get the money.'

'What are you talking about? The police don't let people out on bail; the courts do that.'

'So do the police. And if we go and get it, they'll let him go while they're making further enquiries.'

Surely he couldn't have got it wrong, so few minutes ago. 'You mean – you mean we've got to go all the way back to Hampstead, then back here, then back to Hampstead again?'

He was sucking his thumb. 'Mmmm.'

'Are you sure?'

But he was laughing now, laughing wildly, whether through relief or the look on my face or the sheer stupidity of our journey. ''Course I'm sure,' he said between giggles. Then, after another burst: 'Julian said I was to come back on the train alone.'

'Good.'

'But you can bring me in the car if you like.'

'What else did he say? And how was he?' I started the engine wearily. I had learnt little, yet sensed anti-climax: Canter's jubilation was restricted to his having got past the visit to the Station.

'He seemed the same as usual, that's the funny thing. I mean, tired and red-eyed. Or perhaps he was more – you know, resigned than usual. But he smiled and said sorry to bring us here – I told him you had driven me up.'

'In front of the police?'

'No, we were in the sort of entrance hall and this sergeant and the chap who brought him there were chatting in the corner.'

I paused before turning into the main road. We could have telephoned my father and asked him to arrange for the money to be made available at a Stratford bank. But that was bound to involve him, and in any case he had particularly ruled out telephone calls. I waited for a milk lorry to go by, then set off the way we had come.

'You can sleep on the train coming back,' I said. 'I'll take you to Hampstead, then on to the station. What else did he say?'

'Nothing really. Well, just sorry and he hoped it wouldn't do me any harm. "Not as long as they don't lock you up for years," I replied, and then he looked ghastly for a bit and I was sorry I'd said it. He said he'd explain it all once we were home but – '

It was getting light now. I glanced at Canter who seemed to be smiling. 'But?'

'He said – it made no difference to what he felt about me. No difference at all.'

Now we were silent without tension, and not long after we reached the open country Canter fell asleep.

Part of me was becoming wide-awake again but my eyes were aching. The big, fast-moving lorries and the in-between light made driving more difficult; and I resented Canter withdrawing into sleep. However inane his conversation, it would have helped to pass the journey more quickly. I began to long for breakfast and a bath, then bed, glorious bed. We were due for an exciting lecture half-way through that morning, and I had been looking forward to it, but I would only fall asleep if I went. Besides, I would probably be expected to attend the conference at Julian's flat.

I stopped the car on the other side of Woodstock for a pee. Canter woke and peered about him, then went straight back to sleep. But when I pulled up at an all night café beyond Oxford, he managed to wake up and accompany me. Inside it was warm and steamy; and the man behind the counter was friendly. Lorry drivers sat at two long tables, one foursome arguing heatedly about the merits of different braking systems, the others reading news-papers or sleeping. The tea was a bit too strong and the bacon greasy, but we both felt better for our breakfast.

When we reached the flat, I stayed in the car. Ten minutes later Canter reappeared as I was about to fetch him. He had clearly washed (and had probably had a quick, skimming shave); and he waved an envelope at me as he came down the stairs. He had not mentioned the sum demanded by the police and I hadn't asked, though why *that* should have seemed a delicate question I can no longer remember. Mostly I kept thinking how an action that might have lasted anything from seconds to a few minutes (I assumed) was going to have repercussions for years to come. Eliot's

> The awful daring of a moment's surrender
> Which an age of prudence can never retract

seemed very apt (though, truth to tell, I remembered the quotation wrongly at the time).

I dropped Canter outside the station, confining myself to a mutter and a wave. We were both suddenly embarrassed, like two men emerging from a drunken exchange of confidences. As I drew away and headed for Belgravia, I was already aware of the sharp change in atmosphere between us; looking back I find it hard to account for it. Did I feel that I was deserting him? Did he feel that he and Julian had involved me too deeply in their troubles? Or was there a sudden realization on his part that, despite everything, I was an outsider, no doubt critical and disapproving? Canter belonged to that breed of hyper-sensitive homosexuals who simply cannot believe that most people are indifferent to their deviation.

On the way to my father the fourth call box at which I stopped was free. Karen hardly sounded pleased to hear from me at that time of the morning, but was instantly sympathetic when I sketched in Julian's trouble. 'Can *I* do anything?'

'Could you let Molly know? I ought to, but I'm a bit afraid of that woman particularly in this instance.'

''Course I will.'

'And can we meet? Tonight, I mean.'

She paused, then sighed. 'In the circumstances – yes. I was supposed to be seeing Martin but –.' There was a note of amusement rather than regret in her voice; or was I hearing sympathy where I wanted to find it?

'Thank you,' I said quickly. 'I need someone to lean on after the last twelve hours.'

'Thank *you*,' came the quick, colder response.

'The Perco? At seven?'

'Yes – better make it eight. I must go now. *Ciao.*'

'*Ciao,*' I echoed automatically, wondering whether the extra hour was to allow her to meet and dispose of Martin. Catching sight of myself, tired, unshaven, slightly the 'wanted man', in the kiosk mirror, I shuddered. I needed some rest and a bath if I was to compete with him.

My father greeted me calmly while my mother hurried away to make a second breakfast (they had a foreign maid at this period, but to prepare my food herself was mother's way of showing that she was helping). Despite his urbane manner, I knew the old man was waiting to hear the worst. Responding, I pitched straight into the story, sticking to the main details, and querying only the idea of police bail.

'No,' he answered quickly, 'that's in order. There was an Act somewhere round 1925 that established that. In this case it probably means they're short of evidence – unless Julian has said more than he should. We'll know as soon as he gets back.' We were in his study, and he sat with his back to the desk. 'I'm sorry you've got involved in all this, David. It's not very pleasant and you've problems enough of your own already.' (Airy talk or more understanding than I usually allowed him?) My father crossed his legs. 'It's not going to be easy for anyone.'

'Including yourself?'

'Yes. If the story breaks, it would probably spoil my chances: they're very narrow after all. On the other hand, to drop out of the running now might be needlessly throwing the game away: they may decide not to proceed against Julian. Against that – if they do proceed, I may be more permanently damaged by hanging on. Roy's attitude is that I ought not to prejudge my position until we've had the meeting with Julian, but I'm not sure these legal laddies understand the political urgency. One astute policeman at Stratford and the story might break at any moment.'

I nodded unhelpfully since there was nothing I could add to this inner debate.

'In one sense I can't blame Julian, though he might have restrained himself at this of all periods in my life. I don't really believe that he couldn't help himself – we're all subject to wild temptations from time to time. But as often as I tell myself it's unnatural and vicious, I still feel somehow responsible for him.'

'But – '

'No, David, don't protest. People need help even when they don't ask for it directly. Besides, your grandfather – who knew nothing of the special circumstances as far as I know – commended your uncle to my care. It was among his last wishes and was witnessed by the whole family.'

I think it was at that moment that I realized he was talking his way round to something; and his next sentence confirmed it. 'I was saying to your mother a bit earlier that what we don't know is whether the police would drop the whole thing if I went up to Stratford and vouched for Julian. Of course, I'd have to resign from the race then.' He looked at me as though for an answer, but fortunately my mother called to say that breakfast was ready.

fourteen

MY FATHER and Roy Gater arrived first; and we began to wonder whether Julian and Canter would get there before my father had to leave for the House. Roy kept asking me questions about the College, which is how adults think they're showing interest in a young person. But when he said, for the third time: 'So you're living here?' I began to wonder whether he was asking some unspoken questions as well. My father must have come to the same conclusion. 'In view of my position,' he said, 'we thought it better for David to live away from home.'

Roy was an old friend as well as his solicitor, and they had known each other before I was born. So I thought that the time had come to set the record straight. 'I'm not queer, if that's what you're thinking,' I said in a more aggressive tone than I had intended.

'David!' My father stood up abruptly. 'Whatever could – '

'Your vagueness mainly,' put in Roy. He was a large, well-dressed man dominated by a huge moustache. His size and ex-RAF flying-officer appearance camouflaged a good brain. 'I must admit I was beginning to wonder.'

'Of course you weren't,' my father blustered.

'I can't see why it would be so much more shocking in your son than in your brother, but I'm delighted it isn't – naturally.'

My father was walking about the room, and I had the feeling that he was going to protest further. Fortunately the arrival of a taxi took his attention; and he momentarily relaxed as he saw Julian and Canter get out. Julian stood looking at the ground while the actor paid the fare, then he noticed my father's car. He looked cold and, even from this distance, unshaven, and for a moment I had the feeling that he was contemplating running away down the road. But when Canter took him by the shoulder and steered him towards the steps, he smiled fleetingly and complied. It was only when they entered the room a few moments later (we three were then standing in the fixed formality of a tableau) that I realized how haggard he was. He nodded to us all, then sat down.

I introduced Canter to Roy Gater, who seemed to have been infected by my father's contempt for the actor: his tone of greeting contained a built-in dismissal. If Canter was offended, he didn't show it. He poured a large whisky for Julian, then asked the rest of us what we wanted. As he continued to pour drinks, my father became self-elected chairman.

'I can only spare you a few moments as I'm due in the House soon, but Roy will stay on to discuss the details. However, there are one of two things we must establish from the outset. Have you been charged? And if so, what is the exact wording of that charge?'

When Julian failed to look up from his glass, I began to think that my father's callous, business-like approach was the last straw in a series of humiliations. Something, though, in the way Julian sipped his drink suggested that he had already had a number before reaching the house; and a woolliness in his diction seemed to confirm my guess.

'Well?' My father was poised for anger or ready-made sympathy.

'I'm not sure,' said Julian. 'I didn't say anything if that's what's worrying you – or not much.' He looked at his brother now. 'They're accusing me of indecently assaulting a young boy at the hotel.'

'Did you?' asked my father quietly.

'If I may interrupt,' said Roy quickly, 'we're going too fast. Julian's clearly had a nasty shock and it would be stupid as well as unkind to press him too hard on this. May I suggest that you go off to the House, Mark, and you –' he nodded at me, then Canter – 'leave us alone for half an hour.' He looked at Canter again. 'It's not, of course, a matter of secrets or anything like that. It's simply that Julian may find it easier to answer my questions alone in the first place. Then later on we could meet back here to discuss the situation with all the facts in front of us.'

My father looked impatient, and I half expected him to insist on immediate discussion with everyone present. Then he shrugged his shoulders and stood up. 'I've already wasted a lot of time I can ill afford at the moment, so perhaps you're right. I've got a dinner this evening and there's likely to be a division in the House about ten. I can't see myself getting back here much before eleven.' He looked challengingly at Roy.

'Shall we say eleven thirty?' replied the solicitor. 'You won't have to rush then.'

It seemed to me then (as it does even now) that I was missing all sorts of overtones to the conversation. My father and Gater were using formulae beyond my reach. I mention this not because subsequent events revealed anything that I had missed, but because there was an air of complicity between the two men. When we discussed it a few days later, Canter agreed with me but Julian thought the overtones part of our imagination. I can't help feeling, though, that had the crucial discussions taken place then and there, the outcome for everyone might have been happier.

Roy's proposal was put into operation without further discussion. My father offered me a lift into town, though I had no intention of going to the College; and Canter disappeared to his bedroom. Julian seemed further saddened by our departure (or perhaps it was only Canter's he resented), and I felt sorry for him. This feeling was magnified when I described the scene to Karen in the Percolator that evening.

'It's so unfair,' she repeated, tugging at her hair as she spoke. 'The punishment's out of all proportion to the crime.'

'Hold on,' I said. 'This wasn't the usual score you're always going on about with consenting adults as the only people involved. Julian seduced a young innocent boy.'

Karen looked at me wildly. 'For crying out loud, David, do come off those emotive words! How do you know the boy was innocent, as you put it? And how many *innocent* boys have ever been perverted because they've been seduced once, twice or ten times? I've been to bed with two boys who'd had considerable homosexual experience through coming under the influence of queers when they were thirteen or fourteen, but that hasn't dented their adult performance one bit.' She spotted her dormant spoon and beat me to it. 'You're like one of these nannies,' she said laughing. 'You repeat yards of emotional prejudice untested by a shred of scientific evidence. For all we know, it might have done the wretched child good!'

'Now you're being ridiculous,' I protested, weaning the spoon away from her by stroking her hand.

'Why? We know from psycho-analysis that all males go through a homosexual stage. Getting it through an experienced grown-up may be better for the child than having a smutty experience with a kid of his own age. Oh David, don't look so stupidly shocked all the time! You're getting like your old man with all this pseudo-puritanism. Playing with a little boy's joystick can't be so shattering a thing that it can justify ruining a man's career – let alone spoiling your father's chances of becoming PM. This really is a case of inherited and environmental taboos run wild.' She looked round the crowded coffee bar (a young couple at the next table were listening to her with fascination), then back at me. 'Even if the boy was corrupted – and that's pretty well impossible without pre-disposition towards inversion – but if he was, how can you equate this with people dying of lung cancer or the Bomb or road deaths? It's tiny in comparison, and only frightening because it brings out the beast prejudice in most men, repeat men. Women are rarely involved in all this.' She withdrew her hand and let herself lean back against the leather-padded bench seat. 'But what's the use? You're as boss-eyed as the rest.'

I was, too, but not in the way she thought. Inwardly I knew that she was right, although she was probably overstating her case. But something stopped me from admitting this. Did I, perhaps, resent having this explained to me by a girl? Or was it that while the intellectual in me agreed with her, instinctive taboos ruled at a lower level? I glanced at the couple at the next table. They smiled and I smiled back, not sure where their sympathies lay. Had they heard the whole conversation? Did they know who I was then, and that the man we were discussing was my uncle?

I switched back to Karen. She was pushing a few grains of sugar round the bottom of her cup. 'How the hell do you know all this?' I asked.

'Stock answer number five when you don't like what you're being told.' She laughed. 'You know, David, what I'm saying isn't something madly esoteric. It's something you'd learn in an elementary psychology course – or even in a liberal arts talk on the subject.'

Much as I resisted her dogmatic way of lecturing me, I had to accept that she seemed sure of her facts. Could she really have learnt all this at school? Or was she rapidly acquiring the knowledge at the hospital? Certainly it began to seem that she had chosen the right job; and with that thought I remembered Molly.

'Did you tell Molly about Julian?'

'I did.'

'What did she say?'

'She flatly refused to believe it. There are lots of people jealous of his success and this is an attempt by one of them to discredit him.'

'To which you answered?'

Karen reclaimed her spoon. 'That I had no idea whether people were jealous of him or not, but I thought it pretty unlikely that anyone would go to such lengths to compensate for their jealousy.' She sighed. 'I nearly said a whole lot more, but remembering that she'd got me the job, I managed a "still, we'll see". Not that that satisfied her.' Karen smiled. 'Drawing her voice up to its full height, she swept off the telephone with the remark that she was very well placed and would have immediate enquiries made into the whole thing!'

'God forbid!'

'Why?'

'Because the less publicity the better. The next few days are crucial for the old man, and the tiniest whiff of scandal could sink him. As it is I saw somewhere that Bradley had – ' I broke off as I became aware that Karen was no longer listening. Instead she was watching someone over my shoulder.

'Is that the boy who's supposed to have given that story about us to the paper?'

Without turning I checked in the long mirror to see who she was looking at. It was Grant Dellon.

'Yes.'

'Martin pointed him out to me the other night, but he couldn't speak to him as he was with two other boys, all three camping it to high heaven.'

Grant had ordered a coffee and was now moving away from the counter with it. He saw that there was room at our table and started to walk towards it, but as he drew level, he recognized me.

He stopped, turned and sat down where he was, two tables from us. I was watching all this so carefully that I didn't see Martin come in, get himself a coffee and cross to join us until I heard his 'may I?'

'Do.' I tried to sound neutral. After all we saw each other most days. We rarely spoke and never mentioned Karen, but there had been no quarrel. As Martin reached for a chair from the adjoining table, I put my hand on Karen's.

'I see our friend's back,' said Martin, nodding towards Grant. 'It's time we had a word with the rat.'

'If it was him,' I said.

'Let's find out,' answered Martin; and before I could deter him, he got up and made his way to Grant's table.

Karen watched him admiringly. There was about her an air of excitement, almost of mischief. Had she arranged that Martin should join us at The Percolator? What excuse had she given him for not keeping the original date? I was tempted to ask questions out loud, but Martin came back with Grant in tow.

'You two know each other, I think. Karen, this is Grant.'

'Hi!'

Martin neatly caught another vacant chair with the toe of his right foot and slid it up to the table. Then he sat down on the other side of Karen while Grant sat between him and me.

'You weren't in today?' Grant said to me.

'No.' We had not spoken for weeks, but apparently he still kept a check on my movements.

'Helping your father in his campaign?'

It sounded like harmless teasing; it couldn't very well be much more. Unless the papers already had the story of Julian and were holding on to it for the moment; and Grant had heard it from one of his journalist friends. I smiled. 'Only by keeping out of his way.'

Grant started to say – 'I guess that's quite valuable in a – ' when Martin cut in with: 'You're rather pally with the press, aren't you?'

'Two of my friends are reporters.'

'And you feed them stuff about the College?'

'What are you trying to say?' The American had grown taut and defensive.

'I'm not trying to say anything. I'm saying it quite simply. When that article appeared the other day with a photograph of Karen and David in the middle of it, we were told that some of the information came from you.'

Paradoxically, Grant looked relieved. 'Possible,' he said, still a little wary. 'My buddies and I talk like everyone talks and no one's going to go into class every day with a future Prime Minister's son without mentioning it.'

'No?' Martin looked threatening and powerful, but he achieved this without changing his expression. It was his natural demeanor when he was not smiling, but now the situation and his own words heightened it. 'Well, just listen to this, Grant. If you feed as much as another word to your Daily Liar friends about either of these two here, you'll be sorry you ever left the States. OK?'

Grant looked defiant and anxious at the same time. 'OK,' he muttered, but I guessed that Martin had done more harm than good. The American should have been handled more subtly, warned off by hint and innuendo: threats would only bring out the feline spitefulness in his nature. Nor was I happy about the effect of Martin's threat on Karen: she sat there admiring him, for all the world like a mediaeval maiden defended from a dragon.

'How's your father doing?' asked Martin, running his fingers through his curly hair.

'Still in the running, for what that's worth.'

Martin reached across and took Karen's spoon from her. 'Good.' He shook the spoon at her but spoke to me. 'How come you never dissuaded her from this business of thrashing her coffee by the hour?'

I was about to answer when Grant stood up. He said nothing, but started to move away without looking at us. A moment later he was through the door into the street.

'Well,' said Karen, 'that's put a stop to that.'

'I wouldn't be so sure,' I said.

'How's the trick cyclist?' Martin asked her.

I raised my eyebrows.

'You haven't heard? Karen's fallen for an old, old man, a crummy visiting psychiatrist who analyses her – that's what *she* says – every Tuesday and Thursday afternoon for two hours.' He exchanged a look with the girl. 'How come you kept this a deadly secret from David?'

'*Now* I understand,' I said. 'She was blinding me with psychology before you arrived, and I wondered where it all came from. "Even a liberal arts talk on the subject would have given you an insight into the effect of a violent seduction of a minor by an older person of the same sex,"' I mimicked.

'You're both horrible,' said Karen, little disconcerted.

'All this to do with your uncle?' Martin turned to Karen. 'Or shouldn't I have said that?'

'It's a bit late to ask now,' answered the girl, visibly put out for the first time.

'Why *little* boys?' Martin asked me.

I was annoyed with Karen for having told him at all, let alone for going into details. Surely she could have made some non-committal excuse for cancelling their meeting. 'I don't really know,' I said.

'Either through an early fixation,' Karen explained, 'or the fear of approaching older people.'

Martin shrugged his shoulders in an exaggerated gesture. 'Do you think she analyses us like this all the time?'

'Begins to look like it.'

In the silence that followed I remembered Molly. I ought to phone her or get my father to phone her. In her panic she was capable of speaking to the wrong person and saying the wrong thing. Like delayed shock after a motor smash, I began to go cold at the thought of the damage she might already have done. 'Look, I must go and phone Molly, and try to make sure she doesn't talk to anyone.' When Martin looked puzzled, I added: 'You'd better tell him what it's all about while I make the call.'

I hurried into the street and searched for a call box. Luckily I had four pence with me. Molly's number, however, was ex-directory and I was forced to rely on my memory. Fortunately it worked, and a moment later she answered the phone herself.

'It's David, David Coulsdon here. How –'

'What news?'

'Julian's home, and there's to be another meeting with my father and his solicitor late tonight.' I was wondering how to ask her whether she had told anyone, when she said –

'I've spoken to Desmond Avery. He's willing to help but told me not to mention the case to anyone else until I'd seen your father.'

I felt a great sense of relief. 'He's right. If one word of this leaks into the papers, father's chances are finished.'

'Where are you having this meeting?'

'Julian's flat at half past eleven.'

'I'll be there.'

I was so taken aback by the idea that I thought I must have misheard her, but she added: 'I'll see if I can get Desmond to join us.'

My father – and possibly Julian – would be furious. 'Don't you think it might be better to wait until tomorrow? They'll have got over the preliminary business by then.'

'Are you trying to tell me not to meddle?'

I thought for a moment. 'For the time being – yes. Molly, I don't mean to be rude – ' I heard her slam down the phone. I waited for a few moments in case she had second thoughts, then replaced the receiver. 'Blast!' I said aloud and kicked the side of the box. A girl outside, waiting to follow me, stepped back as I came out.

Karen and Martin were deep in conversation when I entered the Percolator but they stopped talking as I sat down. 'Well?'

'I've made a bigger mess than ever,' I explained. 'Molly's going to join this meeting between my father, his solicitor and Julian later tonight. And she's bringing that lawyer, Desmond Avery.'

'At least he's sympathetic,' said Karen.

'I'm beginning to believe it's too late for sympathy. Nothing short of a miracle will save Julian – *and* my old man – the way things are shaping.'

I left them a few moments later. Originally I had planned to stay with Karen until eleven. When Martin had turned up I was even more determined to see her to the Tube myself. But in taking the initiative to inform Molly, then doubling that error by telling her of the meeting, I had created a debt to Julian. I could repay a little of it by forewarning him. Was that the only reason that I told them that I must be going? Probably not, because it was from that evening that I dated my feeling that I had lost out to Martin where Karen was concerned.

fifteen

I FOUND Julian at home alone. This was not, after all, so strange, yet not for one moment had the possibility occurred to me. That Canter would never leave him alone in the present crisis seemed a truism; that he might have sent the actor on an errand did not cross my mind. Most of us talk airily about homosexuality, the seduction of minors and similar objects. Faced with someone deeply involved in one of them, the confidence sags. I stood at the drawing-room door embarrassed and tongue-tied.

'Come in, come in,' said Julian, 'I won't bite you – or worse.'

'Where's Canter?' I asked before I could stop myself.

'Gone to his beloved club. Oh, I know what you're thinking. How could anyone be so heartless and inhuman? In fact it's the opposite. He just can't stand the suspense of not knowing what's going to happen to me, and must do something to take his mind off it.'

'OK.' I answered harshly. 'So he's all right. But what about you? Don't you count?' I moved to the armchair opposite him. 'Or is there some special twist in all this that I've not latched on to.'

My uncle smiled. 'No, David, not really. But selfishness doesn't exclude love. We pretend that love means making sacrifices for the other person; and often that's true. But selfish people are capable of love, even when they're hell bent on getting their own way.'

'Point not taken,' I replied laughing, 'but at least it's got us over my shyness. Sorry.'

'Don't apologize. If this gets out, the pattern's going to be repeated all along the line. It's easy enough for liberals to sympathize with adult homosexuals who are victims of the law. But with kids – even they shudder.'

'Except Karen.'

'Why Karen?'

'According to her that line about it doing great harm to kids is crap. Unless they've a predisposition to your sort of slant, the experience just slides off their backs like water.' I lowered my voice. 'Do you believe that, too?'

Julian made great play of lighting a cigarette, and as he began to watch the smoke drifting towards the high, patterned ceiling, I began to think he was trying to let the question dissolve into it. But then his gaze swung down at me. 'I haven't any views either way,' he said slowly. 'I don't suppose I've ever stopped to consider it.' He began gently nodding his head. 'Naturally I prefer it if the kid enjoys it too, and I know whether he does or doesn't; but for the rest I'm neutral.'

I hoped that he wouldn't ask me whether I was shocked. I was – and puzzled as well. That night when he had told me about his particular perversion, he had been explicit that until then it had been a mental one. Now he spoke as if it had happened on numerous occasions. But before I could ask for an explanation he was talking again.

'Now you bring the subject up, David, you remind me of the cock-eyed way society looks at this sort of thing. They always assume it's the man who seduces the boy, but you know, many a time it's the boy, oh yes, twelve, thirteen, fourteen years of age, too – it's the *boy* who actively seduces the man.' He paused. 'Certainly that's how it happened at Stratford.'

I wanted to hear and not to hear; to know what, how, how far; and where it went wrong. And all at the same time I wanted to change the subject, to be able to deny that Julian, my Uncle Julian, had ever had anything to do with the whole grisly business. It was too late, and yet I still wanted to hear him say: you know, David, the whole thing's a ghastly mistake. Of course I looked at the boy – even winked at him; and what was going on in my mind was nobody's business. But I can assure you I never so much as laid my hand on his shoulder. Instead, he said:

'It was Henry IV, Part I, last night. And it took off, every little bit of the production jelling and adding to the exciting total impression. I came out singing – metaphorically speaking – and started to wander towards that queer pub. What's its name? I've forgotten for the moment; anyway it doesn't matter. And then suddenly I knew that was the last thing I wanted. At best I'd pick someone up and it would all be pretty sordid; otherwise I'd be frustrated. Either way I'd kill the mood.'

'But you wouldn't find schoolboys in a pub?'

'*Schoolboys?* Oh, I see. No, of course not. I'm not only interested in schoolboys, much as everyone would like to conveniently label me pederast and shove me in a pigeon hole. I like older people, too, chaps of Canter's age' – he paused almost imperceptibly – 'and yours.'

I was sorry to have diverted him. I had become curious about the main story and wanted to hear it in Julian's own words. But it wouldn't be long before my father and Roy Gater arrived.

Julian cocked one leg over the arm of his chair. 'So I wandered back to the hotel, tossed up about having a drink in the bar and went on up to bed when the coin came down tails, which meant no drink. The corridors are long – do you know the place? – and they were quietly lit and deserted. I passed a bathroom just before reaching my bedroom and the door (it had slipped open although the bolt had been half engaged) was a few inches ajar. In the tub was Christopher (Oh God, David, even the most beguiling name of all), naked, exciting, excited and smiling at me.'

If I have succeeded in conveying the slight quality of lyricism in my uncle's words I have still not given any indication of his tone. It might have been a connoisseur describing an exquisite painting in his collection; a lover becoming rapturous about his girl-friend; a traveller facing for the first time the glory of the Alps or Dolomites. Julian's tone had become dreamy, his attitude languid, and I knew, at that moment, that what he was regretting was not his precarious position, not even the possible dangers for my father: it was the loss of this pretty schoolboy.

'He saw me standing there, rooted to the spot and speechless, and he beckoned. Nothing crude, mind you, no hooked finger or waving arm. Just a raising of the eyebrows and the most gloriously evil, inviting smile that any flaxen-haired, fourteen-year old beauty has ever worn. And in I went, succumbing instantly and completely and marvellously. What is more, David, and more extraordinary, I knew what I was doing; knew that it was lunacy and could only end in tragedy. And yet I went on as if impelled by an inevitable fate; and, you know, I still think that I was – and always will think so. What probably sounds like a sordid little story to you was a moment of truth for me; and not all the courts and policemen and tuttings of lawyers and your father can dim that conviction for a thousandth of a second.'

Julian stopped talking, and we were left in a deep, separated silence. I had rushed home to tell him about Molly and had not mentioned her. I was anxious for my father's future and determined to make my uncle see the dangers. Yet all this paled before a feeling, something more than a premonition but less than a certainty, that Julian was mentally ill. His regrets were lip service, his repentance nonexistent and his mind, senses and concern tightly wrapped in the madness of a quick, chance encounter with a stupid schoolboy. If my father tumbled to this situation, all was lost. I had precious little time in which to save it.

'Molly's on her way here,' I said brutally. 'She's trying to bring Desmond Avery with her.'

'Don't solicitors engage barristers, then?' So different, so matter-of-fact and straightforward was Julian's tone that I was once again left feeling that I had dreamt the previous conversation.

'*You* know Molly,' I answered less heavily.

'I'm afraid so – at least sometimes. Who told her?'

'I did – through Karen.'

'She, too? Who else knows?'

'I'm sorry, Julian,' I said, shy again. 'I panicked a bit when we got back from Stratford.'

He held up his hand. 'Against the proportions of my sins, yours are trifling. Forget it. At least you feel sorry for your tiny slips. I only regret the way I ballsed up the most fabulous encounter of my life.' He lit another cigarette. 'I used to ask myself why the ultimate was always flaxen-haired and blue-eyed. Connolly's got a thing on this type business in *Enemies of Promise*. Good book, that, though I don't think it's in print any more. Where was I?'

'Leading up to telling me exactly how you got caught.' The bully was creeping back as I began to believe that he was acting, holding me at arm's length and trying to prevent me making any judgment.

'You know, David, when you think how easy it is to get killed – just cross the road at the wrong moment – or for a plane to crash or a war to wipe out a whole population, what a lot of fuss we make about a man of my age running his hand down a boy's spine. Don't we? We get so worked up about it that we never stop to ask why? Or how? Your father finds himself, if that's an OK expression, by cohabiting with your mother. I do the same by hugging a flaxen-haired little boy. But why? Why *that* boy with *those* eyes and *that* heavenly mouth? All boys are roughly the same, aren't they?'

I heard my father's car stop outside and felt a sense of relief, only then realizing how tense I had become. If Julian had simply been off his rocker it would have been easy: I could have rung for a doctor. But possessed as he was, and no other word quite describes the trance that moulded his words and expression, there still seemed to be traces of truth and perception muddled into his dream. A madman is capable of the profound, but there had been nothing significant in my uncle's 'Don't solicitors engage barristers, then?'; just a simple exhibition that on one level he was as much the sensible stockbroker as ever. And once my father had entered the room I was at a loss to fix, even in my own mind, the extraordinary lyric, disjointed mood that Julian had so recently projected.

'Roy not here?' If my father felt embarrassed, nothing showed. He looked tired and pale, though.

'How did things go?' I asked.

'In the House? Fine. In other ways it has become more complicated than ever.' My father paused as Julian stood up. I thought that he was going to interrupt with a fervent apology, but it was to offer us, without speaking, a drink. 'Bradley's approached me with a compromise: he is to become PM, myself Foreign Secretary and my eventual succession to have his full support.' He waited for our comments, but Julian was busy with a bottle of whisky and I had no idea whether such a compromise was good or bad. 'Julian – before Roy arrives – did you do what they're accusing you of – last night, I mean?'

As soon as the question had been asked Julian reverted to the shrunken individual who had climbed out of the taxi with Canter that lunch time. Now, hesitantly squirting the soda into a glass, he was victim and criminal. There was no longer a trace of the debonair or lyrical, only a worried old man who'd nastily interfered with an innocent boy.

'Yes and no.'

'What does that mean?'

Julian handed us our glasses. I don't like soda in whisky but hadn't the heart to protest. 'I did talk to and – ' each word was costing him an effort – 'and touch the boy but not – not anything more – not what they say.'

'What do they say?'

This, I knew, was the form of interview my father had wanted that morning. Denied this triumph by Gater, he was seizing the good fortune of having arrived first. Watching the two brothers in profile (they faced each other now that Julian had resumed his seat), I was reminded of nothing so much as the man who rubs a dog's nose in its own dirt and tells the world it's for the animal's good. Of course it is, but this in no way excuses the glee with which it is done.

Outside, another car could be heard. Gater? Molly?

'Well?'

'They say I indecently assaulted him.'

'How?'

I was certain now that my father was enjoying it. All forms of power were grist to his mill, even the petty, sadistic bullying of his own brother. He was already more awake and less worn looking, and this could hardly have come from the first sips of whisky.

'He was in the bath,' said Julian doubtfully.

'And?'

But Gater, without ringing or waiting, had taken advantage of the unlocked front door, crossed the hall, knocked and entered. He looked fresh compared to the rest of us, accepted the offer of a drink and stood by the fireplace, at once in command.

'I've been to Stratford,' he announced, 'and had a word with the boys there. They're not too keen on pressing a charge for half a dozen reasons, but Christopher Lowell's father is. I doubt whether they'll dissuade him either.' He took his glass from Julian and

smiled neutrally. 'It seems the boy's had a fair amount of experience of this sort of thing at school, and the Inspector – off the
record, naturally – thinks that he may even have been involved
with an adult before. And, of course, the hotel would like the thing
played down, and the Inspector's sympathetic there. But if this Mr
Lowell insists, they've got no choice but to go on.'

'Can they prove it?' asked my father.

Gater looked at him in surprise, glanced at Julian, then looked
back. 'I should think so.'

I dreaded my father asking how, for Julian seemed every moment
to be shrivelling in his misery. But instead he said: 'When shall we
know?'

'Lowell is seeing his own solicitor tomorrow morning. That'll
probably be the turning point.' He stopped at the sound of a car
outside and cocked his head on one side. 'You expecting someone
else?' he asked Julian.

My uncle made a noise that could have been 'yes' or 'no', so I
said: 'I'm afraid this is my fault;' and knew by their expressions that
this was the first time that my father and Roy Gater had really reg-
istered my existence.

'How come?'

'It's Molly Rapton. I stupidly told her what had happened as
she's very fond of Julian, and she insisted on coming along.' I could
hear voices now. 'And bringing her friend, Desmond Avery.'

'Who's Molly Rapton?' demanded Gater, clearly annoyed.

'The wife of Lance Rapton, the publisher. She's a sociologist and
a meddler.' My father turned to me. 'You should never have mentioned this meeting to her.'

'I know.' The bell rang, and I hurried to answer it.

Molly wore an expensive-looking fur coat and looked slightly
feverish. The lawyer seemed ill-at-ease, though he smiled pleasantly enough when he recognized me. I stepped back to let them
in, and Molly marched straight to the lounge. When she threw
open the door, Julian could be seen getting up, then making his
way to the bookcase, his back to her. My father and Gater stood,
but that did nothing to offset a clear antipathy to her arrival.

'Do you all know one another?' she asked imperially as she

crossed the room, glancing back to nod towards Avery. There were ambiguous murmurs followed by slight bows or movements of the head. I stayed at the door waiting for either my father or Gater to explode. But it was Avery who spoke.

'I tried to convince Molly on the way here that our visit would at best be impertinent. In any case I only came as a friend.' (Of Molly's? Or Julian's? My uncle mechanically pulled volumes from the shelves then pushed them back with sharp, exaggerated movements.)

'Mrs Rapton, we all understand and share your concern, but by the nature of things at this stage it would be better if our discussions were confined to the smallest number of people possible. As a matter of fact I was about to ask my son to leave us when you arrived.'

Molly now stood near enough to my uncle to touch him, but she had not once looked in his direction. 'Julian would never harm a soul,' she said in a cold, hard tone, speaking as if she had heard nothing of my father's words.

'That's not the point at issue,' answered my father. 'Mrs Rapton, you would help enormously by leaving us at the moment.' He turned slightly. 'Wouldn't she, Julian?'

My uncle kept hold of the spine of the book that he had just replaced, as if hanging from it. When he spoke, his voice was surprisingly gentle. 'I'll ring you tomorrow, Molly, early in the morning.' He moved the upper part of his body so that he could face Avery. 'Thank you for coming with Molly, but the whole thing's out of my hands now. My brother and Mr Gater are running it.' He shrugged his shoulders and turned back to the bookcase.

'That's what I mean!' said Molly, looking steadily from one to another (but leaving me out). 'You're all worried about Mr Coulsdon's reputation, but what matters is Julian. He's the one who's got to go on living with this from now on, true or false. That's why I came.'

Avery crossed to her and took her gently by the arm. 'I think we ought to go, Molly.' He turned to Gater. 'If, later on, I can help, you'll no doubt contact my clerk.'

'Thank you'; but there was no enthusiasm in the solicitor's tone.

Molly moved a step nearer Julian, Avery's hand still on her arm. 'If only you'd come to my dinner, none of this would have happened.' The lawyer must have increased the pressure of his grip. 'All right, all right, I'm coming. Julian, don't let them persuade you into admitting things you didn't do just to get peace. *Please.*' She began to move away, the lawyer leading her.

'Thank you, Molly.' Julian's voice was high pitched. 'Goodnight, Mr Avery.'

I accompanied them to the front door. On the steps first Molly, then the lawyer asked me questions, and I told them the current position. They then left, roaring down the road in Avery's Jaguar. When I returned to the drawing-room, my father curtly suggested that I leave them for half an hour. I shrugged my shoulders, and complied.

sixteen

HE WAS *just disappearing into the bathroom as I rounded the corner. I only caught a glimpse – woolly dressing gown tightly tied at the waist, mop, and I mean mop, of blond hair falling over his forehead. I stopped dead where I was. I could hear the bath water running and him whistling, but no click of a bolt or lock. Then there was a sound of wood scraping. He must have knocked into a chair or something. The whistling ceased and a moment later so did the water. I hadn't moved a pace along the half-lit, narrow corridor with its dark walls and sloping floor.*

My heart was racing as if I'd run a mile. I rushed forward, grasped the handle and threw open the door. He was standing in the bath, small but every bit of him perfectly formed, and in the middle of his oh so smooth brown skin a white patch where he'd worn briefs all summer. For his size he had wide shoulders and a narrow waist, and a firm, rounded little bum that I could have kissed as he stood there. All this in a second, for he swung round and smiled at me, not shy or put out. He had one of those flat, open, English faces, slightly upturned nose, sensual mouth and the whitest of teeth. All this and that cleft at the top of his little bum that sent shivers down me.

'Hullo,' he said in a cheeky Public School voice. 'Who are you?'

As if hypnotized, I came in and shut the door behind me. He was soaping his smooth thighs and went on unconcerned. I felt hot and giddy, and kept trying to say something. In the end I held out my hand and touched his back, and he moved round towards me and I could hardly believe it: he was excited already.

There was a noise in the lounge or corridor and I dropped the diary back on the desk. I was appalled by what I had read and appalled at myself for reading it. After my father had suggested my leaving the room, I had stood for a moment in the hall, tempted to eavesdrop on the conversation from which I had been excluded. But the doors were thick, casual overhearing almost impossible and to be caught with my ear pressed to the pannelling, unthinkable.

I had been about to retire to my own room when I had noticed a light under Julian's door. I had been surprised at this, as I had not heard Canter come in. I knocked quietly. There was no reply, so I opened the door and looked into the room. It was empty, though the ceiling light, the lamp by the bed and the one over the desk were all alight. And the desk was open.

Leaving the door ajar, I strolled into the room. There was nothing in it to interest me except the desk, but I walked slowly round, examining with exaggerated care the bedside table, the books on it and the reproductions on the walls. But I came, ears on the alert, to the desk at last, and idly began to finger the open, quarter-leather bound minute book that lay on it. *He was just disappearing into the bathroom,* I read, then raised my eyes to stare into the blackness outside. Then I had lowered my head again and started to read in earnest, stopping only at the noise in the corridor.

I shut the book with a snap and ran lightly to the door. Someone was coming in to the house. As I waited to see who it was, I glanced back to the desk and realized that I had stupidly closed Julian's diary instead of leaving it open as I had found it. It was too late, though, to correct my mistake since at that moment the front door clicked shut. A second later I heard someone coming up the stairs. Relieved that it was not Canter, I decided to re-open the journal at the page I had been reading and leave the room.

I put my head into the corridor to check that the conversation was still going on in the lounge, then hurried back to the desk. Flicking through the pages to look for the place, my eyes caught other entries.

Back from a fortnight in Capri last night. We both enjoyed it, Canter more than me. On the beach next to the Grade Field's pool, a small, dark, bright-eyed Italian schoolboy used to come and talk to us every day.

Other entries were less equivocal:

Madame Butterfly *with de los Angeles at the Garden last night. Would have thought her too old, but she was heavenly.*

Or:

Finished The Leopard *at last. Marvellous sense of the family and home all crumbling together. Tragic that it wasn't published during the author's lifetime.*

Until, five minutes later, I was back at *he was excited already*. I forced my eyes to the bottom of the page and up to the next one, seeing but not reading the words. Then the words *the moment of truth* caught my eye, and I read on, oblivious to everything else.

He stood by the bed naked again, running his hands along the sides of his flat stomach, then moving to stroke his bum. 'Christopher,' I kept repeating like a madman, 'Christopher, Christopher, Christopher.' And he never stopped smiling that same mischievous, knowing smile. 'You're hooked and you know it, and you know I know it,' it seemed to be saying as I pulled off my own clothes.

I paused and turned the page to see how much more there was and discovered two further sheets of the recklessly scrawled confession. I turned back to *my own clothes*, and started to read on.

'Twice naked.'

I swung round at the words. Julian stood in the doorway, his expression – there is no other word that will match it – *relishing* the situation. Shaken and blushing, I put down the journal. 'I'm terribly sorry,' I began weakly.

'For reading it? Or for me?' He crossed the floor, picked up the book and pushed it firmly to the back of the desk. Then he shut the lid, brought out his keys and locked it.

'I saw the light and thought Canter was here, and came in, and before I knew where I was – '

'You started to read the naked truth.' He laughed self-mockingly. 'I was writing it not long before you arrived, then decided to have a drink. You got back before I could lock it up again.'

'But Julian,' I protested as my confidence returned, 'it's madness to commit this sort of thing to paper, surely?'

'Because it doesn't tally with what I've told you or Gater?'

'No, because it could be used as evidence against you.'

'By whom?'

'The police, of course.' Was he purposely being stupid as a substitute for anger at my behaviour? Or was there some inviolable quality of innocence mixed up in his particular perversion?

'You mean they'll come along, raid the place and seize all the doubtful poems and photographs; then search for – what's the technical term? – pictures of male frontal nudes? Was society ever crazier than when it made it an offence to send such photographs through the post?' He shrugged his shoulders. 'Lance once told me that you could have a book illustration of a negro's prick or a black girl's breasts, but if either subject were white, the author and publisher would be dumped into prison. Perhaps policemen and judges don't have pricks.' We had been standing on either side of the desk. Now he took a pace towards me. 'Where were we, David? I mean, before the frontal nudes business. Oh yes, I know – my diary. I suppose it does represent a tiny risk, but just imagine the greater one of having no record of the incident.'

'I'm not with you.'

He looked at me quizzically. 'I know you're not; and you wouldn't much like it if you were. You see, to you and those two in the next room, what I did was dirty or criminal or both. To me it was a heaven-sent moment of bliss. And I want a record, a detailed moment by moment record, so that if I never have an experience like it for the rest of my life, I can still go back to those words and re-live it.'

I was beginning to doubt his balance of mind again. No strictly sane person would talk like that. On the other hand, no really insane person would exhibit the fears and nerves that showed through his apparent equanimity. Perhaps he was both: insane in his perversion, sane in all else. But how did one force him to understand that society would never accept this balance? How could I make him see that the price he would have to pay was astronomical, and that others, like my father and Canter, would have to meet some of the bill?

'You're going to preach a sermon, David, I can see it in your expression. And you're too young for that. Morality is what suits the dominant majority, and so I'm immoral. I don't pretend otherwise. But not, young man, in my own eyes. If you can't understand that, there's no point in further exchanges between us.' He jerked his head at the desk. 'What is more, it becomes your duty to take that journal to the police.'

'Julian, are you unhinged or something? Don't you see that your actions are not isolated from the rest of the world? They affect that boy, they affect Canter and they affect my father.' I lowered my voice. 'It's not an abstract question of moral beliefs. The law exists, and you have broken it. For Canter's sake and my father's sake your offence must be minimized. Doesn't that make sense?'

'On the assumption that my integrity is expendable, yes. But it's not. If you're motoring at thirty miles an hour in a built-up area, and get stopped by the police and charged with doing fifty, do you lie low in order to "minimize the crime"?'

'But that's different.'

'In *your* eyes – and so back to square one.'

We stood by the desk in the huge bedroom staring at each other. I could in a way understand *this* uncle, defensive, proud, obtuse, but what of the one who had cringed away from Molly and kowtowed to my father? Why did *I* bring out a defiance that was not exhibited to others? Somewhere on the edge of my consciousness hovered the memory of a Ruskin Spear interior I had once seen: a large, saloon bar, Victorian décor, and in the background, two people; a big, blowsy woman and a small, perky man. My uncle was that man; the woman was all the forces against him, forces that would end by disfiguring him in one way or another. It might make sense for an invert to repay society's bias by rebelling, but society remained the brick wall against which the invert's vulnerable head could only be dented.

Julian moved self-consciously towards the bed, then flopped down on it. 'Anything is good if the pursuit of it pleases somebody and does not increase misery,' he intoned quietly. 'That's a fair basis for an honest morality, isn't it?' He looked up at me and shaded his eyes against the centre light. 'That's let me out, because I enjoyed it in the deepest sense.' He lowered his hands and closed his eyes. 'That leaves Christopher. Kant said we must treat people as ends in themselves and never as a means to our own ends. How did he go on? "Lying and stealing are wrong, sexual exploitation is wrong, because these things mean using other people as a means to our own ends."' Julian sat up and opened his eyes. 'But Christopher didn't just enjoy it, he encouraged and provoked it every inch of the way. So it was good for him, too.'

'You're working hard,' I said neutrally, 'but not convincingly.

The kid may have enjoyed it, but how do you know what long-term damage you've done to him?'

'I don't, and nor do you. All the high-falutin' judges' *spiel* at the end of trials is just a typical piece of unscientific prejudice. It's like the old one about dirty books corrupting the young. Have you ever met anyone who has been corrupted by a book?'

The tone of bravado held to the end, but I suspected that the word 'judges' had touched off another thought. He seemed to wince, and a moment later began to crumble. He let himself fall back on the bed again. 'Turn out the centre light,' he said so quietly that I only just made out the words. I did as he asked, then remained standing by the door. 'David.'

'Yes?'

'I don't want to go to prison,' he whispered urgently. 'They can't send me there, can they? I mean, they haven't real proof, have they?'

I was sorry for him, but no longer that sorry. 'Since I still don't know what they might have real proof of, I can't answer that question.'

We were silent; and I guessed that he would squeeze the rest of the story out of himself given time. But at that moment a door opened and my father called. 'Julian! David! Would you come in, please?'

I went out of the room without even checking to see whether Julian was following. My father and Roy Gater were sitting where I had left them, so I took the upright chair next to the fireplace. Julian delayed a moment or two before following me, and I began to wonder if he had run out by the back door. I recalled his fugitive look when he had stepped out of the taxi with Canter that morning. Then he came slowly, defensively into the room, inconceivably its owner.

I expected Roy Gater to propose the next steps, but it was my father who spoke. 'It seems almost certain, Julian, that this Mr Lowell will press for an action. If so, Roy feels that we ought to enter a plea of not guilty – there is no actual proof, after all – and with luck you'll get away with it altogether. At the worst, though, you may be found guilty of some minor indecency charge, and fined.'

'Still – with luck,' said Gater.

My father nodded without conviction. 'The chances of your going to prison are small, which is one relief.' His voice and manner changed, a Chancellor of the Exchequer moving from small-time allowances to major tax changes. 'Roy is also certain that I shall be damaged in one way or another, once the case becomes public; and with the odds as they are, counsels me to throw in my lot with Bradley.' He paused a shade histrionically. 'I shall accept his advice.'

Even if the workings of Fate appear to be running against him, it must be a terrible moment for an ambitious man when he rejects absolutely his chance to win. Yet there was little more in my father's tone than a desire to punish his brother, and I was left feeling that there was even a small measure of relief in having the decision made for him. Perhaps, too, he was more than ever conscious that a refusal to run now might strengthen his chances later. And yet I did at that moment feel sorry for him.* His next words, though, cut short that feeling.

'Your behaviour, Julian, is quite inexplicable. Not only have you, at least temporarily, damaged my career, but you have probably put an end to your own: it would be unthinkable for you to remain in the partnership once this becomes public. And all for what? To indulge some very unpleasant and sordid little vice which any decent man would shudder at.' He stood up magisterially. 'I have no doubt that I am much to blame for this. Ill-advised by others, I accepted your cohabiting with this actor-fellow as if it was – well, almost normal. And this, I am sure – ' he turned momentarily to the solicitor – 'and Roy is inclined to agree with me, this encouraged you to grovel to the depths.'

'Oh father, chuck it!' I spoke almost despite myself, but immediately seized the advantage my interruption had created. 'Don't you think Julian's going through hell enough without your pious canting? Have you forgotten – '

'David, how dare you! I blame myself for ever encouraging you

---

* Readers of A. J. P. Taylor's brilliant book on the crisis of that time will know how misguided this was; but at the time it seemed likely enough.

to live in this house.' He fingered his chin as if thinking. 'And I expect an immediate apology for this unfortunate outburst – due no doubt to your tiredness.'

I got up and left the room. It was stupid to argue and stupid to apologize: I could only hope that my intervention had taken the pressure off Julian. Poor Julian! Men lusted for power and killed; men engineered wars and destroyed, and my wretched uncle had touched a boy's bum (or whatever), and was being made into a pariah for it. Disgusted, I retired to my own room and waited for the summons that would surely be a prelude to a further scene. But ten minutes later I heard my father and the solicitor leave the house; and I rejoined Julian in the lounge in case he needed help. Almost immediately Canter came in.

'That was well timed,' I said.

The actor laughed. 'I've been outside for the last half an hour, waiting for them to go.' He went up to Julian. 'Have they been hell, pet?'

'They would have been but for David here. He jumped at Mark as soon as the main sermon started.'

'Good for you!' said Canter. 'So where do we stand?'

'Gater thinks the boy's father will force a prosecution, but if we play it down, I'll only get fined.'

'Good.' The actor helped himself to a drink, then winked at my uncle. 'Stick it out, boy. You may still get away with it. Don't *you* think so, David?'

'I don't really know,' I answered. 'I'm not even sure what Julian did.'

'As if it matters. But I'm in the dark, too, when it comes to kids. Why a boy, Julian? Did he look nineteen or like me or something?'

Since I had come back to the room, Julian had been neutral. There was no sign of the whimpering, self-pitying victim nor of the defiant, chest-beating innocent. It was plain, everyday Julian, a little sadder than usual, a little more subdued. He was still wearing the grey suit and dark pink shirt in which he had come back from Stratford. And his tie was made of knitted silk – and black.

'Why boys?' he echoed. 'Sometimes I wish I knew.' He stared at the ceiling as he spoke, occasionally glancing down, but never directly at either of us. 'Some people are supposed to get fixated at that stage of their development, but how do you explain Canter then? Or Desmond and Paul and Silvio who came before Canter? Others say it's a fear of approaching older people. In my case the same people and a dozen or two one night stands rule that out. And what about Norman Douglas, who was married and went to bed with women right into middle age – and still loved boys? Or Gide?' He looked at me. 'I'm not citing names as an excuse,' he protested. 'Only to show that simple rules don't work in this sort of thing.'

'But when did it start?' Canter pressed. 'I've never seen you looking at schoolboys.' Although the actor's curiosity was driving him on, he seemed to be treading warily, watching the effect of each word before adding the next.

'What a mess I've got you into by letting you move in here,' Julian said to me suddenly. 'It seemed rather fun to begin with, partly because we like you and partly because – '

'Yes?'

'It added zest to the situation having an outsider living here.' He closed his eyes and shook his head vigorously. 'Sorry. Where were we? Oh yes, when did I start fancying little boys? Always and always, I suppose. Right back to my first private prep school I got crushes on one after another. I can remember their names – and their faces – even now.'

'Yes,' I said, 'but we all went through that stage.'

Julian laughed. 'No you didn't, chum. Yours were Romantic Crushes. I wanted to crush the little devils – and it was always the devils, never the angels – in my arms. And at some trifling age I became expert in squashing them in the Tube and the changing-rooms, and, when opportunity offered, in the showers.'

'But you didn't get a hard-on or anything?'

Julian smiled at Canter. 'Not in the earliest years, no. But by the time I was eight or nine . . .' He shrugged his shoulders.

Once more I found the details repulsive. As long as these con-versations stayed on an abstract level, I could agree with Karen that peoples' sex lives were their own business. But this constant mental masturbation made me feel sticky. Although my feelings for Julian since living with him had altered like a barometer on a gusty March day, the basic sympathy and liking remained. But just as I had no desire to know the details of his daily visits to the lavatory, so I could have done without so much of the scabrous detail that seemed part of homosexuals' lives.

'And you've had boys?'

'Not between school and this week.'

'Never?' This was my question, and I surprised myself by asking it.

Julian yawned. 'God, it's late; and I'm whacked. And I suppose Gater will be on to me at five minutes past dawn.'

Canter stood. 'It's time we all got some shut-eye,' he said. 'And me for a pee first.' He ambled out of the room.

Julian jumped to his feet with an alacrity that belied his fatigue. 'David,' he said, 'would you do something for me?'

'Depends.'

'No conditions. I'm asking for help.'

'All right.'

'If I put my journal in a sealed envelope, would you take it home and lock it in one of your drawers till this has blown over?'

I had expected worse. 'Of course.'

'And swear not to read it?'

I thought for a moment. 'Yes,' I agreed slowly.

'And never, never tell anyone what you read in it tonight?'

Again I agreed.

'Especially not Canter.'

From the corridor came the sound of the lavatory being flushed.

seventeen

KAREN and I had lunch in a café near the hospital. Even in those days I used to wonder whether cheap cafés in other countries were as dirty and dowdy as our own. Most of my travelling abroad at that time had been done stylishly with my parents. But two forays into France with fellow students had shown me that there at least you could eat well in cheap places. In England the tables were almost always wet, the vegetables soggy and the meat stringy. Today was no exception.

The room was crowded with office juniors, van drivers and some of the manual workers from the hospital. Apart from three long tables, there were four small ones, and I had managed to secure one of these on arrival, pushing away its third chair to ensure that we were left alone. By the time that Karen arrived, the café was full and it was all I could do to keep her chair free. She looked hot and somehow subdued, but I was so full of my own news that I didn't pause to question her. Instead I plunged straight into my story.

'But how did you get the note?' she asked as I neared the end.

'It was delivered by a messenger. I don't know whether he came from the Ministry or was hired specially. Canter opened the door to him and I didn't get a glimpse.'

'And that's all it said?'

I nodded. '"Your mother and I have decided that it would be better if you were to return home to live immediately. We shall expect you before evening" – or some frigid nonsense.'

'Of course you're not going to obey?'

'That's my girl! Just what I wanted to hear you say.' I was pleased that she was backing me even before I had shown my hand.

After we'd ordered soup and steak pie, Karen said: 'There's no danger in your staying on there?'

'What's that supposed to mean?'

She took a hunk of bread offered us by a fat woman who seemed to be the only waitress (later in the meal I noticed that most of the regulars fetched their own food), and began to break it into bits, adding her own crumbs to those already littering the table. 'You're not a bit like that yourself, are you?'

'Bloody hell!' I answered angrily. 'What *is* the matter with you?'

Karen smiled. 'I didn't think so but Martin said he'd heard it.'

'Who from?' I demanded. The room was noisy with chatter and clatter, but one or two people glanced round as I shouted, then turned back to their own plates.

'A girl called Rosemary told him she knew for certain.'

'Bitch!' I said, as the fat woman banged plates of soup in front of us, adding quickly: 'That's what Rosemary is,' in case the waitress thought I was referring to her. 'Anyway, what are you supposed to be? A queer in drag or something?'

Karen started to stir her soup, then: 'No, just rather boyish-looking according to the same source.'

'That's not coffee.'

'The subject *is* making you irritable, isn't it?'

'Wouldn't you get angry if I said people were saying you were les?'

'Not really, because I know I'm not.'

'Anyway, perhaps I'd better tell you what started Miss Rosemary Carlos in this particular bit of treachery, and we already know what motives Mr Bensted has, don't we?' I paused, but when Karen said nothing, I started on the story of my meetings with Rosemary.

Karen stayed silent for a few moments after I had finished, then – 'Why did you hold back then? Particularly if she's as attractive as you say.'

'Are you still on about your precious Martin's theory?'

The empty soup dishes were exchanged for plates of steak pie, fluffy potatoes and squelchy cabbage.

Karen picked up her knife and fork. 'How, David Coulsdon, you ever had the cool, bloody cheek to sulk at my going out with Martin when you were trying to make this Rosemary, I just don't know.'

I suppose I could have explained. But what? That I wasn't queer? That I hadn't touched Rosemary out of feeling for her? But I had protested enough or, nearer the truth as I can see from this vantage point, I was becoming disenchanted of the snub-nosed, sexy girl. If she really wanted Martin, then I would bow out.

'Look,' I said, tussling furiously with a piece of tough steak, 'if you want Martin, fair enough. I've enjoyed what's been between us and I'm sorry it's over, but if it is, that's that. Don't let's have me smeared with stories about my being queer to help put an end to it. 'Cause I'm not, and you know it.'

Karen sighed deeply. 'Why must everything be so cut and dried? What's wrong with just drifting along and enjoying it? I like Martin and I like you, but if either of you is going to become possessive about – '

'So he is, too?'

Now she laughed gaily. 'May I change the subject?'

I nodded, at the same time taking her hand in mine. Half of me wanted to go on quarrelling, to have it out, to punish her for having the best of both worlds at my expense, but the other half knew that the price was the end of the relationship. This one lunch had probably done more harm than all the previous differences put together; even careful handling would only produce a temporary reprieve.

'Why don't you find a room on your own now?'

'What do I do for money? Father would stop my allowance on the spot.'

'Won't he anyway, if you refuse to go home?'

Probably, I thought, but it would matter less. There was no rent to pay at Julian's; nor did I contribute to the cost of food and drink. Did my father? I'd never given the matter a second's thought. If so, he could hardly stop paying as long as I was there. But there was another reason, harder to formulate but no less powerful for that: to move out was to let Julian down. Had I ever got into trouble he would have helped me. It was the least I could do for him.

'Molly would like to speak to you,' said Karen when she could see I was not going to reply. 'She phoned this morning.' So after lunch, without warning her in advance, I went round to the Raptons.

The maid told me that madam had been to London Airport

to meet Mr Rapton, had taken him to his office and returned so exhausted that she had gone to rest. The explanation was meant to drive me away. I replied that somehow during that rush of events Mrs Rapton had sent me a message that she wanted to see me urgently; and here I was. I had no doubt that as soon as she knew I had arrived, she would come downstairs. Although I had been bluffing and the maid on the point of doubting me, two or three minutes after she had gone upstairs, Molly came into the study.

I had spent those minutes carrying out a rapid inspection of the room. I was a little disappointed with the result, though I'm not sure what I had expected to find. There was a pile of unopened mail addressed to Lance, but otherwise the big desk was empty of everything save telephone, paperweight and photo of Molly. I was somehow disappointed, too, in her appearance when she hurried into the room. I had not, it is true, expected a great tragic act. Perhaps I had, though, anticipated her being somewhat distraught or despairing. Instead she was the usually self-possessed, commanding Molly.

'I hoped you would call or phone this afternoon,' she started, sitting in the armchair by the window and indicating an upright chair by the desk for me. 'What's the current position?'

About my father? Or Julian? The wrong answer would incur her contempt. 'They're waiting to see whether the boy's father insists on the police prosecuting.'

'And if he does?'

'They hope he'll get away with a fine.'

'Why all this "hoping"?'

'I'm sorry but I don't understand.'

Molly spoke slowly, as if to a child. 'While I was at London Airport waiting for Lance – his plane was twenty minutes late – I managed to get through to your father. He told me that Julian was absolutely not guilty. It seems that he was attracted to the boy in a vague paternal way – he's always wanted children of his own, you know – and harmlessly fondled his neck.' Molly brought out the words as if she was reciting one of the juiciest bits of *The Tropic of Cancer*. 'The boy was so full of the smut drummed into him by older boys at school, that he alleged all sorts of other things and is now too frightened of being called a liar to withdraw his allegations. So what "hoping" has to do with it, I don't understand.'

Nor did I, though my puzzle came from a different angle: was my father misleading Molly or had Julian successfully misled him? And how far was my own knowledge informed by what Julian had told me and by what I had read in the journal? If Molly believed what she was saying, why had she wanted to get in touch with me so urgently? A truly innocent Julian hardly needed the employment of panic measures.

Whether she paused to give me a chance to reply or to enhance the air of drama she was giving to our meeting, I don't know. But when she started speaking again, her voice was darker, almost conspiratorial in tone. 'Since you can't express what is surely in your mind, I will. Innocence is not enough. The child is young and appealing, Julian is a bachelor and living with a homosexual. Also the provincial police are often vindictive in these cases. So there is a real danger that Julian may get entangled in the law.' She raised her eyebrows questioningly.

'Definitely,' I said, since on this at least she had my agreement.

'What is more, once a charge is preferred, Julian will have to resign his partnership. He will be without a job and at the mercy of an unsympathetic or wrong-headed judge.' She sat back in her chair, a queen propounding her plans to a young courtier: certainly her expression matched the metaphor.

'That's where you come in, David.' She glanced round the room, then pointed to a silver cigarette box on the bookcase ledge. 'Pass me a cigarette, please.'

With a mild show of reluctance I did as she asked. I resented the way this ex-Jewish publisher's wife turned everyone into a servant. Sociologist nothing, I thought as I held the box towards her; it would be better if she learnt some simple, everyday manners. Then I settled back to hear whatever ludicrous scheme had taken her fancy.

'Julian must leave the country at once. On the one hand his departure can be announced to his partners as necessary for his health (after all, it follows on logically from his trying to stave off his – what shall we say? – *nervous* troubles by going to Stratford for

a few days).' She smiled at her own ingenuity. 'On the other it can
be conveyed to the police with a tacit understanding that he will
not re-enter the country for a year or two. This will almost certainly dissuade them from bringing a charge, besides helping them
to turn a blind eye to Julian's breaking bail.'

My antagonism lessened in face of her proposal: she seemed
to have a better grasp of the possibilities than either Gater or my
father. 'Can the police turn a blind eye in that way?'

'According to Desmond – yes.'

(So she had already taken the precaution of checking her scheme
with the lawyer. Or was it his?)

'I don't know whether you know, but Lance and I have a small
villa on the outskirts of Le Lavandou. I would suggest that Julian
goes straight there. We have a woman who looks after it and we
can warn her by express letter to have it ready; and I myself will be
going down there in a week or two. I always do at the beginning
of the winter, then again at Christmas. When he has had a chance
to see how things work out, Julian can take further decisions.'

'I must say you've got it all tied up,' I said with enthusiasm. 'But
where do I come in?'

She smiled again, this time more warmly. 'It won't be easy to
persuade Julian – '

'But surely it will! This would save him – and my father – a mass
of troubles.'

'No, David, nothing is as simple as that. If I know Julian, his
reaction will be that Canter depends on him and he can't desert the
man.'

'Then why can't Canter go with him? He's not working – '

'NO!'

I was amazed at the indignation of her negative.

'That wretched man would drag him down all over again – and,
anyway, if I know him, he just wouldn't go.' She waited to see if I
would agree, then went on. 'I believe that you and you alone can
persuade Julian to do this despite Canter. He wouldn't listen to me,
nor to your father, and certainly not to lawyers. But he might to
you. And you must try – and keep on trying until he's on the plane
to Paris or Nice.'

She stubbed out her cigarette and folded her hands on her lap. She had finished.

I was with her all the way except the doubt. How could Julian fail to respond to an idea that would ensure his freedom *and* keep my father's reputation intact? He must after all care about my father. Or did he? Had he said anything that clearly showed this? He seemed sorry for the trouble he was causing and sorry – for himself. But he was fond of my father. At least, I supposed so, as one conventionally does in such cases. But supposing he wasn't, supposing he was jealous of my father and his career and his wife and – his son! But I was getting ridiculous.

'Well?'

I hadn't realized that Molly was waiting for an answer. 'If I fail?'

'You mustn't! I'm warning you, David, that whatever the logic of our plan, Julian won't accept it without a struggle. Don't forget that I know him very well, very well indeed.'

I wanted to ask: 'Supposing Canter wants to go with him,' but echoes of her shouted 'No!' checked me. Instead I said: 'You're sure he wouldn't listen to you even more than to me?'

She leant forward slightly, but relaxed nothing of her authority. 'At the moment he's running away from me because he thinks I'm judging him. It would be nearly impossible for me to strike the right note. Besides, I'm very fond of him, and the strength of my plan is its logic. It's much better that it should be put forward by someone less involved emotionally.'

She stopped as if another thought had crossed her mind, opened her mouth as if to voice it, then shut it again.

'Do I tell him that it's your plan?'

She considered that for a moment. 'No, just say we were both very concerned about him and it grew out of our conversations.'

I stood up. 'Then I'll try to get hold of him this afternoon.'

She smiled encouragingly. 'Yes, do, please. And phone me the minute you have some news.' She held out her hand, shook mine warmly and added: 'Thank you, David.' But she never moved from her chair as I left the room.

There is a bizarre quality about Hampstead that I had always found difficult to fix, but I caught it as I walked down the High

Street that afternoon. The people who live there *are* intellectuals, but they are also self-conscious of their roles; *are* bohemian but dress for it as though on the stage; *are avant-garde*, but appear to have seen the colour supplements the Sunday before they are published. Watching and walking, I was seized yet again by lassitude at a moment of crisis. I stopped to look in shop windows; saw a crude, flattened copper cross on a chunky necklace chain and wondered whether Karen would like it. Then I strolled into the High Hill Bookshop.

The pattern of the street was repeated. These people cared about books but were self-conscious about their caring. The shop, though, was casual and in the groove. In half an hour I had mentally bought a twelve guinea book on Chagall and a six guinea one on Beato Angelico; and physically a five shilling paperback on Mondrian. Seeing a student from the College come into the shop, I glanced at my watch, then cursed myself for dallying for so long. Having paid for my book, I hurried away to Julian without speaking to the girl, though we knew each other slightly.

Julian and Canter were at home. At the time I don't think I would have dared to describe the atmosphere in that room when I breezed in: it would have sounded soppy and sentimental. Nowadays I'm less self-conscious. They looked and sounded like lovers, tender and warm with each other, sitting together on the couch, Julian's arm round Canter's neck.

'What news?' I asked after refusing a cup of tea.

'The prosecution's on I'm afraid,' answered Canter quietly.

'You've been charged?'

Julian shook his head. 'No, Gater phoned to say that the boy's father was adamant. Gater's going to see him tomorrow morning and the police will wait till then.'

I hardly wanted to broach Molly's plan in front of Canter, but now it was more urgent than ever. 'I suppose this'll mean you're resigning in the City?'

'No doubt about that,' Julian answered, while Canter added: 'But we'll manage just the same. My agent's pretty certain he's landed me a comedy part in a new TV serial.'

'Good,' I said. 'Julian, why don't you get away?'

'What do you mean?'

'Leave the country for a time. They'd probably drop the charge altogether then, and you wouldn't have to resign your partnership. You could say you'd had some nervous trouble and been medically advised to go abroad for a few months.' Was it their blank expressions? Or did I lack the authority of Molly's voice?

Julian disengaged his arm from Canter's shoulder. 'What the hell are you burbling about?' he said. 'Where did you dig *this* up?' He frowned. 'Not Mark, it wouldn't be his idea of behaving decently; and I've spoken to Gater this afternoon.' He turned to Canter. 'I think I've got it,' he went on, smiling at the actor, then facing me again. 'You've been got at by Molly. Right?'

'Right,' I agreed, 'but she's got something.'

'She certainly has. If I were to say "yes", she'd have achieved her wildest ambition – to part Canter and me.' He put his hand on the actor's. 'I'm surprised that you were taken in by it, David. Very surprised.'

I was annoyed now, annoyed with Molly for involving me and annoyed with Julian for being so obtuse. 'Better to be separated that way than by your being sent to prison.'

'You horrid little boy!' said Canter, only half humorously. 'There's no question of that.'

'And what did our Molly suggest I do for money? Put in an application to the Bank of England?' Julian winked at Canter. 'To the Chief Cashier: I, Julian Coulsdon, hereby apply for ten pounds a day of French francs to assist in exporting myself out of reach of the British Law.' He winked again, this time at me. 'Or is Indecent Assault an extraditable offence?'

It was difficult to go on, but I could hardly make matters worse. 'Molly says you can have their villa at Le Lavandou. That would cut your expenses quite a bit.'

Julian turned to Canter. 'She's got it all worked out, our Molly, and this schoolboy here laps it up sip by sip. I bet she even told him that within a few weeks she'd come down to help tuck me up at nights.' He raised his hand as I went to interrupt, facing me as he did so. 'I'll take another bet, David. She told you she always goes down there at this time of the year, so it would fit in nicely.'

There was no point in answering. They knew from my expression that Julian was right. I was getting angry, too, partly at my uncle's careless rejection of the lifebelt he had been offered, partly at their indulging in physical endearments in front of me. But still aware of the urgency of Molly's plea, I made one further attempt.

'Why don't you just go away then, both of you? Surely you've got enough money to live quietly abroad for a few months? Then, when it's all blown over, you can come back.'

Julian studied me carefully before answering. 'There are lots of reasons why we can't,' he said at last, 'but the main one is the simplest: once you start running away in this sort of situation, you're never allowed to stop. OK, so I've blotted my copybook. Then let's pay for the mistake – as lightly as we can – and start again from scratch. Isn't that so, my pet?'

For answer Canter squeezed his arm.

His obstinacy spurred me to attack. 'How do you know you're not being self-destructive à la Oscar Wilde? I've always understood *he* could have got away if he'd wanted to – and look what misery he could have saved himself and his wife and kids.' I stood up, crossed to the window, then looked back at them. 'After all, even in this case it's not just you who stands to lose.'

'That,' Julian said to Canter, 'is the King of Trumps. Please explain your hand.'

I had gone further than I had intended. Mention of my father was now inevitable, and with it the issues at stake would be changed. But why not? If Julian, deluded by his new-found unity with Canter, was not clever enough to save himself, then any way in which I could bring pressure to bear on him was permissible. A teacher at my first art school preached the use of fair or foul means to get people to look at pictures; after that, he said, the paintings would do the rest. He was, of course, over-optimistic, or so I've since learnt, but two converts in a hundred were worth the effort. My odds were much longer.

'My hand? Surely I don't have to tell you father's still in the running to be the next Prime Minister, do I? He's got a hard enough struggle as it is without having to face – ' Canter's look bit me off, but the last three words had hardly been audible anyway.

'The additional hazards of the scandalous behaviour of his younger brother?'

'Thank you.'

'Don't mention it,' Julian beckoned. 'Why don't you sit down? Glooming out of the window like that, you remind me of *my* father whenever one of us had done something wrong.' He waited until I had returned to my seat. 'Thank you. Now – what you're proposing is that I set my moral convictions against your father's career; and having done so, plump for him. Or do I have to agree first that he would make a good Prime Minister? You wouldn't after all want me to sacrifice my integrity for a bad one, would you?'

Canter looked as though he wanted to cheer, while I became steadily angrier. For crying out loud, I wanted to say, I'm on your side, and yet you treat me as though I was one of *them*. All this talk of integrity is sheer eyewash. Our duty to ourselves is to live our lives to the fullest extent of our potentialities: the rest is hypocrisy. But I knew this line would only lead to a row. And I knew my mistake now: I should never have spoken in front of Canter, whatever the urgency. Consciously or subconsciously Julian always played the hero for him.

'Watch his expression, pet. We've had the King of Trumps; now for the Ace.'

'Are you surprised?' I heard myself saying. 'You can't go abroad and save yourself *and* my father because you can't be parted from Canter. What about this being at the end of your tether when he stays out half the night?' As Canter made to protest, I faced him. 'And all your attempts to get me to connive at your goings-on behind Julian's back? Do you think I'm going to believe in this sacred union stuff you've tarted up for the occasion? You'll need a better excuse than that for destroying everything father's built during God knows how many years.'

Canter shouted: 'You little horror!' and, almost simultaneously Julian demanded what Molly had done to me; but their expressions showed neither anger nor horror; and I knew I had lost. I had made enemies of them both for no good reason, and all because, as Julian had put it, Molly had got at me. Curse it, and curse her!

'Look,' I said, 'sorry about that, but you two sitting there looking smug as purring cats are calculated to bring out the worst in anyone.' I got up again and started to walk about. 'Surely I don't have to tell you I want to help you, do I? But just because Molly's an infatuated, scheming bitch, it doesn't mean she hasn't got the right idea. You agree with that?'

Julian nodded, while Canter mimed impatience.

'And no one can accuse me of being number-one standard-bearer, but you have no right to expose father, whatever his aptitudes to become PM.'

'No man is an island,' said Julian, still unruffled.

'What's that now?' Canter asked.

'Donne pronounced Dunn,' I obliged, taking the opportunity of reducing the temperature a little.

'Sorry, David,' said Julian after a slight pause, 'but you're way off beam, boy. If you're right about Canter and me when the weather's fine, it has nothing to do with what happens when a storm blows up. Everybody becomes less selfish in those conditions.' He motioned me back to my chair. 'Mark's more tricky. Of course I don't want to spoil his chances – he didn't choose to have a queer brother after all. But I honestly believe that in the long run I'd be a bigger traitor to him by running away than by staying and seeing it out. And our star of stage and TV here agrees with me don't you, darling?'

Canter's 'yes' was simple and strong, and finally convinced me that there was nothing more to say. He must have sensed this because he announced that he was going to start on the supper; and left the room without waiting to see whether I would answer. Whatever her qualms, Molly should have spoken to Julian herself. Or had she known that it would be hopeless? She *had* warned me how difficult it was going to be. Just the same, I held the whole thing against her. We had lurched towards a row and somehow skated past it. Julian looked and spoke equably. And Canter had sounded pleasant enough when he had asked whether I liked minestrone. But the scene had been live, not tape-recorded; and the words I had spoken could never be erased. Canter only tolerated me in any case; but I had lost the friend in Julian. Only the uncle remained.

It was the uncle who reminded me of the favour I had promised. 'I've got that Journal neatly packed up. Would you take it
home tonight?' I must have looked surprised, because he added:
'You *did* say you'd hide it for me for the time being, didn't you?'

'Yes, of course, but I wasn't reckoning on going home this
evening.'

'But Mark told me.'

'That he'd ordered me to live at home again?'

'Yes.'

'So he did – but I'm not going.'

Julian considered this for a little, then asked: 'May I ask why?'

What could I say? Because of the complicated political situation;
because I resented the timing of my father's demand; or because I
wasn't a pawn to be shoved here or there the moment they thought
I was being threatened by danger? There was slight truth in all
these, but much more in my feeling of loyalty to a friend who was
down. Only I couldn't have said this to his face at any time; and less
than ever now I had been disloyal to him about Canter.

Did Julian guess any of this? His next words showed that he
might have done. 'Well, will you just take it home and then come
back here?'

'Certainly,' I said, relieved to offer help but worried at the
thought of the inevitable row with my father. Still, with a bit of
luck he would be out: my parents weren't often at home unless
they were entertaining; and that would be as good as being out.
'I'll go as soon as we've eaten.'

'You'll find it by your bed innocuously wrapped in Selfridge's
paper. OK?'

'OK,' I said, but I was less happy when I set out with the green
paper parcel after supper. The meal itself had gone smoothly.
Canter had chattered about the comedy series he hoped to join
and the other actors already in it; he even gave a brief description
of a harmless incident with one of them at the Gay Sailors Club.
The only serious note during the meal was when Julian wondered
aloud what sort of job was still open to him. Canter's 'we'll find
you a walk-on part in the series, duckie,' switched us quickly back
to the chatter plane.

Instead of the Tube, I had caught a number two bus from Swiss Cottage, probably to delay my arrival. At the time I just thought that it was a nice night, crisply cold and starry, an evening of promise. This barely definable feeling of the world at one's feet was so strong that I telephoned Karen when I left the bus at the bottom of Grosvenor Gardens. It was one thing to admit that our relationship was at an end, another to concede total victory to Martin.

At an end, did I say? She sounded so pleased to hear my voice that our inconclusive lunch might just have well have taken place a month earlier instead of that very day. She asked questions about Molly, drew out the story of Julian's reactions to the escape plan and wanted to know what I was doing at the moment. 'Why don't you come out here as soon as you've seen your father?' she asked.

What could have happened, I wondered. Had she quarrelled with Martin? Or been snubbed by him? An invitation to Ealing was a rare enough privilege at the best of times. 'Your people out?'

'No,' she answered (laughing?), 'and if they were, the answer's "no" at this stage of the month.'

'Jesus H. Christ!' I said. 'Can't they hear you?'

But all she said in reply was: 'See you when you get here.'

It was all so unexpected that I was bemused for my first few steps into Belgravia. Only as I neared the Square did I become aware of that alien feeling the district always gave me. It was like venturing up the drive of a large private house: I felt like a trespasser. Despite his accent and manner, my father was not a landed Tory; only a good middle-class one, born and brought up in Addiscombe. The move to Belgravia had come quite late in the day, though as far as my mother and father were concerned, no one would have guessed this. Somehow they both possessed that chameleon quality of reflecting their surroundings and company. I didn't. And tonight my fear of a row enhanced my habitual discomfort at the well-bred streets and haughty houses.

The maid let me in and hastened to tell me that there were guests (her eyes had made an inventory of my corduroy trousers and roll-neck sweater before she had properly opened the door). I slipped quickly up the stairs and into my bedroom, opened the bottom drawer of the wardrobe and slid the parcel between some rarely worn shirts. Then I hurried down the stairs again. My father was waiting in the hall.

'Ah, David, good evening. So you got my note? Good. Mr and Mrs Bradley are dining with us. If you'd like to put on a shirt and jacket, you can join us for coffee.'

'I'm off to see Karen,' I said, not sure whether to row now or tomorrow.

My father looked disappointed. 'We'll see you in the morning then.'

'Look, this isn't the time to talk about this, but I can't leave Uncle Julian at the moment. Canter's in and out all the time and Julian must have someone to support him. Once it's all over, I'll move home again.'

The drawing-room door opened and my mother appeared in the doorway, making urgent signs to my father to rejoin the party. 'Coming, dear,' he said as she turned back into the room; then to me: 'I am astonished at your defiance, David. You are no longer a child – nor, may I add, are you an independent adult. I do not propose to let this pass. Please give it a second thought and speak to me in the morning. Goodnight.' He marched into the drawing-room without waiting for my answer.

Does this happen to everyone around the years sixteen to twenty-two? Or are there young people who are not constantly misunderstood and misinterpreted? Judging by what I know of my own students at the moment, this seems to be the lot of most people. The parent is loath to see the child strike out on his own however much he protests to the contrary; and the child, so lucid with his friends and contemporaries, always chooses the wrong moment or words with his parents. I was not frightened by my father's threats, but the quick interchange had lapped up half my pleasure in the evening. It took a sharp walk to the Victoria Underground to dissipate my sense of frustration.

I had to wait nearly ten minutes for a train. When it finally came, a gorgeous piece stepped out of the door which stopped opposite me. She was tall and dreamy with deep, moist eyes, lovely legs and a sexy walk that nearly led to my getting stuck in the closing doors. Altogether I had seen her for sixty seconds. A hundred and twenty perhaps; but this encounter completely restored my sense of promise. This was not just at an earthy level, though by the time four or five stations had gone by I had spent at least three long, sleepless nights with her; but she had also re-charged my spirits by the sheer pleasure of exposing them to so beautiful and pleasing a human being.

Karen opened the door to me. She was wearing jeans and an old sweater of mine and her hair was in more of a mess than usual; but she, too, was full of bounce and fun, which made it all the more strange that she took me into the living-room. Her parents received me warmly but they seemed almost as surprised as I was. Every few minutes I expected Karen to suggest going to her room or out for a walk, but we stayed on, half-talking, half-watching a television play and all the time munching *After-Eights*.

At eleven o'clock her parents went to bed.

'Well?' I said.

'Well what?' Karen replied. She was sprawled on the couch, legs thrust forward along the green carpet, head little higher than her body. I thought at first that she had not taken my meaning. Then, maliciously (or so it seemed to me) she said: 'Martin asked me to marry him.'

'And?' I felt all-of-a-sudden dragged right down.

'I thought you ought to be the first to know.'

'You mean you said "yes"?' I demanded. 'You called me all the way out here and stuck me with an evening of telly and your people just to – '

'Ssssh! Not so loud, David!'

' – that you are going to marry that thieving – '

'You *are* getting angry, aren't you? As a matter of fact I hadn't made up my mind before you came.' She smiled (I swear it) guile-lessly. 'But now I have. So wish me luck.'

I did, gracelessly. I could have as easily torn her to bits.

eighteen

SURPRISINGLY Julian and Canter were in bed when I reached the flat. They had not left the hall light on, so perhaps they thought my return unlikely. It was a strange feeling, trespassing again but in a different sense, particularly as one or the other of them had always been up, however late I had arrived. And it was only half past twelve.

I let myself quietly into my room, undressed, then went out again to the bathroom. After cleaning my teeth I had one of those searching mirror sessions: was I so much less handsome than Martin? Was I, well why not admit it, ugly? Or was I below par, and certainly down the league from Martin, when it came to sex? Not even the edge given to Karen's rejection by the bathroom's naked fluorescent could really destroy my confidence in my face. I stood on the edge of the bath, balanced dangerously and took off my dressing gown: nor was that department negligible. Then I realized how stupid I would look if Canter or Julian were to come in suddenly; and hurried back to my bedroom.

Feeling wide-awake I started to draw, easy fluent lines, aimless at first and then gradually hypnotic, the Underground platform, adverts, benches, litter – and the girl. I gave little detail to her, though I remembered her clearly, especially the eyes, but caught the jauntiness of her arrested walk. Then I rubbed out some of the surrounding detail, then more, then more still; and began to reduce her to a feeling, a block, a mass, a sensation of life against flatness. Still wide-awake, I transferred it to a board and painted in some thick, impasto colour in the surrounding areas. But this gave them life. I tried again, brushing flatly for the surroundings, heaping, trowelling the stuff on for the life shape. By half past two it *existed*; abstract to all but me, just recognizable with title, but a realized response to something seen-and-felt. I threw myself on the bed, excited; then paused: or was I deluding myself? Screwing up my eyes I decided not, added a couple of strokes to the shape, toned down a block of cerulean where one of the adverts had stood, and retired, victoriously, to bed. It's not just the hindsight that allows me to add that it proved to be the first of a number of better paintings. The stimulus and situation may have been trite: the painting had, and has, a small life of its own.*

And I liked it even better when I saw it again next morning. After breakfast I showed it to the others: Canter straightaway said 'very good' and was probably quite unmoved; Julian smiled and nodded, and was, I think, impressed by it. It was not easy to tell, though, because an air of expectation hung over the whole meal. Something, in a non-specific sense, was going to happen. The police or Gater or my father would phone, and Julian would need to align his feelings and plans to what was said. An independent decision seemed out of the question; and I felt no temptation to have another try at persuading him to go abroad. Was it, perhaps, then or soon after that I became convinced that he wanted to be (mildly) punished in spite of himself? This might satisfy the conscience he claimed so strenuously not to possess.

Canter fetched the papers while Julian poured us second cups of coffee. On his return he threw down the *Telegraph* so that Julian and I could read it at the same time. The headlines were unequivocal. My father announced that he had no intention of running for the leadership; and that he had never been in the race as far as he was concerned, whatever view some of his valued but misguided supporters might have taken. He had always believed that the party's true interests would best be served by appointing Bradley as their leader. He had little doubt that this would happen within the next few days, but he was not prepared to go as far as to say that he would decline to serve under Corner. And next to the leading double column there was a photograph of the Bradleys leaving last night's dinner party. My father looked sad despite his smile; and my mother looked like a duchess on hearing of a communist revolution in her own country.

---

* It hangs now over my desk in the studio, somehow resented by my wife as she mildly resents everything in that long, lofty room.

'Poor Mark,' said Julian. 'He wanted it so badly.'

I think it was my uncle's sentiment rather than the news itself which spurred me to my next move. 'Look,' I said, 'I'd better move home for a bit. He's got enough on his plate without me rubbing him up the wrong way even if he has got the whole thing lopsided. I'll see him this morning and tell him I'll move tomorrow, if that's all right with you two. In any case I'll have the College after me soon if I don't put in a bit more regular attendance.'

Canter seemed delighted. Before carting the dirty dishes to the kitchen, he carefully admired my painting again. It lay against the back of the couch, a presence in the room, a question and an answer in one. Julian also approved my plan obliquely by praising the painting. 'At least you've done one good picture since you've been here.' He left the table to move the painting slightly.

'Careful, it's wet.'

He turned it away from the direct light. 'How did you come to do it?'

I told him what had happened the previous evening. I spared no one, least of all myself, in describing the row with my father and the off-beat evening with Karen.

'But she's too young to marry,' Julian protested. 'Her people would never allow it.'

I agreed, but knew this would make no difference to the end of our relationship. In any case she had not said when she would marry Martin; and even if they planned to wait two or three years, she would be *incommunicado* to a former lover. Nor would I relish the new role of rejected suitor becoming old friend if it were offered. I would miss her in half a dozen ways, and might have thought it worthwhile to make a life with her myself. But I had let the chance slip; and there was no point in wasting time and feelings regretting it. I must add there were moments of despair and anger. It's hard at this distance to admit it, but half a dozen times I cursed myself for wasting the best years of my life on that girl!

My mother nearly subverted my intention to obey my father by greeting me with: 'I just don't understand you, David, really I don't. To let your father down at a time like this, after all he's done for you . . .' She closed the front door.

'You've been seeing too many "B" movies, dear,' I answered, kissing her lightly on the cheek; but harsh, irrational anger was only just in check.

'And there's no need to use art school language when talking to your mother.'

We stood in the hall by the foot of the stairs. 'And how's "your" father this morning, apart from being top of the pops in most papers?'

Mother retained her dignity by delaying her answer and standing very upright. In those days I was always hearing from other people how much she cared for me and worried about me; and some of her restrictive plans for me might well have sprung from love. But to my face she was never demonstrative, preferring correctness to warmth. Our relationship pertained more to one of those large, rich households where the parents only see their children for an hour a day after tea and the actual upbringing is left to nannies and governesses. 'He needs,' she said sternly, 'your help.'

'And he's going to get it. I'm moving back tomorrow, lock stock and pictures. Where is he now so that I can break the good news?'

'He's being interviewed by a man from the *Sunday Times*, but I don't think they'll be much longer. Have you had breakfast?'

'Mmmm, but I could do with another.'

She looked sorry that she had asked, then told me to wait in the morning-room. She would bring me some eggs, bacon and coffee. 'Good girl!' I said, but she was too preoccupied with my father's difficulties to rise to it. She didn't even turn her head as she marched down the corridor to the kitchen.

For most people morning-rooms, libraries and dens have some special memories. They are often the rooms where middle-class families have witnessed the more traumatic moments of their lives: lacerating parental quarrels, melodramatic juvenile announce-ments, news of birth, death and swingeing bills, for the first post is usually opened in such rooms. But our morning-room in Belgravia was like the house itself: neat, haughty and composed. Besides I had come there too late for it to feel a part of my growing, impres-sionable years. I idled round it now like a stranger awaiting an interview.

My mother brought the breakfast herself. As she bustled with the tray and mats and cutlery, I wondered what the room and house meant to her. Was it ambition achieved? Was this the sort of house that she had dreamed about as a serious, attractive girl in Croydon? Her parents had died while I was still an infant and within a year of each other, and she had been an only child. Had my mother 'done well' in Croydon eyes? Probably, though there were too few of them looking for that to offer much compensation. Compensation for what? I was not sure, but as I looked at her arranging the table, something about the set of her lips and stoop of her shoulders hinted that it was not all exactly as planned. It was the first time that the thought had occurred to me; in later years I never saw her without being conscious of it.

She left me as soon as I sat down, but half way through the meal, father came in. I guessed that she had already told him I was in a conciliatory mood, for he was smiling cheerfully. To make it doubly sure, I plunged straight into the subject.

'Sorry about last night. I hadn't realized that it was a key dinner – and anyhow I was being a bit bloody-minded. I'll move back here tomorrow.'

'Good,' he replied, sitting down opposite me, searching, I supposed, for the right phrase. It was slow coming, so I began to wonder why mother always ran away when she knew that something serious was going to be discussed. Or did he gently suggest that he could handle me more easily on his own? 'I appreciate your apology and the unqualified way in which you have made it, David. On my side I ought to have realized that this hasn't been an easy time for you either.'

'And I didn't want Julian to think I was running away or letting him down,' I added.

The door opened, and mother asked whether he would like some coffee. 'Yes, please, dear,' he answered, then paused until she had closed the door again. 'I in my turn was hasty the other night – and most unfair to your uncle. Since discussing it with Roy again, I have come to see that in the strictly legal sense Julian is innocent. In view of his inclinations his gestures towards the boy may have been exaggerated or over-effusive, but I am certain now that he is innocent of the charge being brought against him, and I am determined to see that he is acquitted of it.'

Did I look as amazed as I felt? I suppose not, since father did not remark on my expression. How on earth had he accomplished this *volte face*? And what was Gater, who must surely have known that Julian was guilty, playing at? I could only assume that he saw a faint chance of getting him legally acquitted and knew that my father would not go along unless assured of Julian's innocence. So I joined the solicitor's conspiracy, if such it was, and said nothing. If my father's price for all-out help was blind belief in Julian's innocence, then I would support that particular bill in my own way.

My mother interrupted to say that a Mrs Standsfield was on the phone for father. He looked surprised but left the room to answer it. 'Isn't that the woman you met at Molly Rapton's dinner party?'

'Yes.' I was just going to expand my answer when my mother remembered that she had not brought a cup and some fresh coffee for my father. When she came back with them a few minutes later, he was still out of the room.

'How are you getting on at the College, David?'

She might just as well have said: 'did you hear that Christ has just landed on the steps of St Pauls?' or 'what about Hitler living in Chalfont St Giles undiscovered all these years?' for its effect on me. Not since I was at a precious preparatory school at the age of six or seven had she so much as alluded to my educational progress.

'I did the first picture in ages last night.' As I spoke I quietly prayed that she wouldn't ask the subject.

'I don't know whether your father's had time to mention it, but we think it might be a good idea now if you had a room or a little flat of your own.' She was standing by the table, watching me carefully. 'Does the idea appeal to you?'

I refrained from commenting on the logic of her thoughts; or the ease with which she had blotted out all memory of my persistent requests for just such a move (two years earlier I would have done so, and probably spoilt the whole thing: adults must be able to believe that they have initiated everything).

Nor, for the same cautious reason, did I want to appear too enthusiastic. 'Yes, I think it might be a good idea.' (spoken slowly to suggest mature consideration). At that moment father came back.

'Mark,' she started, 'David says – '

But he cut across her with – 'One moment, my dear. Mrs Standsfield is still on the telephone. David?'

'Yes.'

'Mrs Standsfield wants you to do her a favour. She's president of a youth club near Tottenham which has been running a competition for pop musicians. The finals are taking place this evening and one of the judges can't manage it. The other three include a television announcer, a jazz critic and a young man who has already had two records in the top fifty. Would you join them as the fourth?'

'Why me?'

'She didn't say and I didn't ask. I presume it was a combination of knowing you and your being young and – '

'And the son of a man in the news which equals the other three celebrity-wise?'

'Maybe, maybe. She also asked me to say that unfortunately she can't be there herself due to other commitments – '

'That's nearly decided me to say "yes".'

'But the judges will be meeting at the organizer's house first, and she will be there for a few minutes to introduce everybody to each other.'

'Why didn't she phone me directly?' I was, of course, playing for time. Did I want to do it? Hadn't I planned to spend this last evening with Julian? When would I pack?

'She did phone you at Julian's, but learning that you had gone out, she thought I might be able to contact you.'

Would it be fun? I wasn't crazy about pop stars or groups, though some of them were all right. Anyway, it would be something new. 'OK,' I said.

My father must have been surprised. 'You mean you will do it?' When I nodded, he hurried out of the room, presumably to forestall me changing my mind.

'It should be rather fun,' ventured my mother.

'You never know. Mother, why don't you come back with me to

see Julian? It would do him the world of good, especially as you're a bit sticky on anything like this in the usual way.'

I might as well have proposed her going down a coalmine or orbiting the earth. Her indignant eyes and lips mouthed, with hardly a movement, a 'really, David!', though she just stood there speechless.

'Well,' I went on, 'I'm doing my good turn tonight. Why not do yours this afternoon?'

There was a further long silence, so that I could only suppose she was wrestling with the traditional batch of conflicting emotions. Mid-struggle father came back, handed me a piece of paper with an address on it and thanked me for accepting Mrs Standsfield's invitation.

'And mother's going to see Julian to cheer him up.'

My father looked pleased. 'Are you?'

She had no choice now. 'Yes,' she said, 'it might do him good to see another face at the moment.'

For a quarter of a minute we were a united family.

nineteen

OFF her home ground, mother relaxed – somewhat. Or perhaps we had got used to each other, for having spent the rest of the morning at the College, I had come home for lunch. My father being at his club, we talked about the Bradleys and the struggle with Corner; and about my father's disappointment. She claimed that this was diluted with relief whereas her own relief was only slightly diluted with disappointment. She would like him to go to Number 10 one day, but wished that it did not involve her in the same journey. Although I knew that she was lying or deluding herself, I nodded sympathetically.

But once in her car she slid perceptibly off her pedestal. 'I'd love a few weeks in some warm place away from everyone and everything,' she confided. 'Perhaps we'll be able to get away as soon as Bradley's Prime Minister.'

'Good idea,' I said, although I knew that this was one of those conversations of the let's emigrate to Italy or bum our way round the world variety, the dreams that keep middle-agers in their same old routine.

'I'll be able to see your picture,' said my mother suddenly, stamping on the accelerator in an unsuccessful attempt to race a much more powerful car down the Finchley Road. 'Did Uncle Julian like it?'

'They both said they did, and I think Uncle Julian meant it.'

We had not telephoned to say we were coming, nor did we know for certain they would be in. As my mother turned into the road, I even began to wonder whether it was such a bright idea. Wasn't there, perhaps, a taint of visiting the accused in his cell? Why should mother today of all days turn up? Quickly alarmed, I expressed my fears to her as she drew up in front of the house.

'Can't we say I've come to collect some of your things?'

'You genius!' I replied. 'Why didn't I think of that?' and led the
way into the house with a lighter heart.

Julian was in alone. He was writing letters as we came into the
drawing-room but quickly gathered them together and put them
under a magazine. He was pleased (I think) to see my mother, but
embarrassed all the same. She had attended too many official cock-
tail parties to worry about that, and was soon chatting away about
my father's sensible decision, Bradley's chances of becoming PM
and her hopes of a brief, distant holiday. At first, while she spoke
and Julian agreed or disagreed, I sat bored but content. But after
a while, my mother's insensitive control contrasted with Julian's
weak complaisance was too much for me.

'Any news from Gater or the police?' I demanded as my mother
for the third time proposed the merits of Marrakesh versus Mon-
tego Bay.

Mother looked affronted but Julian seemed relieved. 'Not yet,
but Roy said he would phone late this afternoon, so I expect we'll
hear soon.'

I looked at my mother, really to see if it was time to go, but
she interpreted it as an invitation to comment. 'Mark absolutely
believes in your innocence,' she said awkwardly.

'Thank you,' replied Julian warmly, 'and thank you for coming.
It was very sweet of you.'

I stood up, and mother followed suit. 'I'd better come with you
'cause my only really decent suit's at home, and you know what
these pop fans are when it comes to clothes.' I turned to my uncle.
'I shan't be in for a meal, Julian. I've agreed to go and judge some
pop thing for Molly's friend, Mrs Standsfield. But I'll be right back
as soon as that carnival's over.'

Julian saw us out, helping me to carry an easel and some canvases to the car. As he waited for my mother to start the engine
and slip it into first gear, he looked up and down the road and once
more his expression suggested a yearning to flee. Then we lurched
forward, he waved, and by the time we reached the end of the road
he was already going back into the house.

'Why don't you call him Uncle any more?' my mother asked as
we entered the stream of traffic going towards the West End. And

the rest of our conversation on that journey stayed at the same level.

Surprisingly mother insisted on my taking the little car when I set off for the pop contest. She told me to keep it overnight and use it for bringing back the rest of my things in the morning. To this day I have no idea what she had felt that afternoon. Was she sorry for Julian? Did she hope that her visit had done him a little good? She was not the sort of woman who gave a clue to her feelings, though whether her character or situation was the cause, I never found out.

I had trouble locating the place that night. Even when I had found the road, I kept pulling up outside the wrong house. Perhaps word association, pop equals modern, led me to peer through the dark for the wrong sort of house. In the end it transpired that Mrs Forster lived in a bulky, Victorian mansion fronted with an enormous bow of a drive. In that drive were a Bentley (Mrs Standsfield?) and a Mini-Cooper (the jazz critic?), a Cortina GT (the TV announcer?) and a white MGB (the pop singer?). I jumped out of the Minor and rang the bell.

Mrs Forster was cute. I loathe the word but almost no other will do. She was fat, but sturdily corseted and poured into a tight teen-age party frock. Above a large, round, not unpretty face she wore a seventeen-year-old's hairstyle; on her feet shoes that would hardly have supported seven stone. 'You're David Coulsdon!' she said in a rich, near cockney accent. 'Come in. This is Phaedra, my daughter.'

I let my feet sink into the thick, latex-lined carpet and shook hands. Daughter was about my age, sultry and sexy. Even then I could hardly keep a straight face at her name or at the hideous 'contemporary' furniture that spiked the eye wherever it looked. Phaedra took my shortie coat while her mother led me towards a long, narrow drawing-room, hilarious with paint. (Was this room and not Kitaj the origin of the British pop art movement?) On the way – 'What a shame, you just missed Mrs Standfield. She told me to tell you thank you for coming and she hoped to see you soon.'

In the lounge, lost in a plethora of orange and vermilion, yellow and kingfisher blue (!), were the other judges (smarter than me), three youth-club leaders (a bit down at heel) and a broad, six foot South American-looking man, whom I took to be Mr Forster, but who turned out to be the A & R man of one of the larger record companies.

To my surprise Mrs Forster made the introductions, poured me a drink and described the procedure. Once over the impact of her appearance, I found her lucid and organized. At 7.45 pm we were to leave the house, at 7.55 arrive at the youth club, at 8 pm take up our positions on a special dais and at 8.5 start the judging. There were two groups in the finals (Phaedra issued us with typed sheets containing the musical history of the groups and brief biographies of its members); we were told how to mark (more typed sheets); and given further drinks.

My second surprise came from the seriousness with which my fellow judges treated the contest. Hadn't I heard the 'Cool-glos'; surely I knew the 'Ragamuffins' disc issued last September? On form to date the 'Ragamuffins' ought to win, but they were a shade weak vocally; on the other hand they were smart in appear-ance and slick in presentation. The other three judges, and Mrs Forster and Phaedra, chipped in with points for or against, occa-sionally spicing their comments with quotations from the Stones, Nat Hentoff, Steve Race, the Byrds, Panassié, Rex Harris and names I didn't quite catch. I laughed, nodded and loudly agreed when consulted. Meanwhile my glass was refilled and the smoked salmon canapés seemed inexhaustible.

'Well,' said Mrs Forster at 7.35, 'we ought to be getting ready.' She turned to one of the youth leaders. 'Will the cars be guarded? Good, then five of us can go in the Bentley; David, you've got your own car?' She swung round to the others (surely one of those overloaded seams would go soon?). 'David's father's the one who nearly became Prime Minister this week.' Pause. 'Mark Coulsdon's his dad.'

The effect of this interpolation in her transport arrangements was ludicrous. It would be an exaggeration to say that everyone sprang to attention, but the effect was the same. You could see that 'and we've been calling him David' look in their eyes. Taking sexy Phaedra with me, I hurried out to the car and waited for the convoy to start.

I asked Phaedra if she had been to all the preliminary rounds of the contest, and she said 'yes'. Did she enjoy this sort of thing? 'Yes.' At this moment the Bentley and one of the other cars moved off; and I followed. I said that I thought a Bentley a big car for a woman to drive. Phaedra said 'yes'. The drinks had begun to convince me that I was quite suited for this pop judging business; Phaedra began to sober me again. So for the following minutes we drove in silence. Then at the next traffic lights we pulled up beside the Bentley. Mrs Forster mouthed something at her daughter through the closed windows. As we returned to our position of number three in the convoy, the girl said: 'What's your dad going to do now he didn't get that job?'

'Go on being Minister of Communications for the moment.' I reckoned that reference to the deal with Bradley whereby he might become Foreign Minister was too involved for Phaedra.

She giggled. 'He don't half say the wrong things sometimes,' she said. 'Like that bit about the minis on Sundays.'

Mercifully we arrived at the youth club. It was a grey, three-storey building with lights in every window. Huge, double swing doors were guarded by two toughs. They were apparently needed, for along the length of the building lounged and leaned thirty to forty grim-faced youths in leather jackets and tight jeans, a few, holding helmets. Apart from them, in nearly identical clobber, was a small group of scrawny girls, two of them with violent ginger hair. By the time I had parked, Mrs Forster was sweeping in through the glass doors, unabashed by the onlookers.

Inside, the hall was packed, thick with smoke and shuddering with noise. Boys with long sideboards and longer hair-lengths talked emphatically with each other or with white-faced, red-mouthed girls. Nearer the front of the large audience, both sexes seemed somewhat gentler, while in the first row were some hot, perspiring, ill-at-ease adults. A path was cleared for us quite brutally by two tough young men, but no one seemed to resent being shouldered aside.

We were taken to a corridor behind the stage and there introduced to the Coolglos and the Ragamuffins. I was shaken by their nervousness and seriousness. They were almost humble as the pop singer wished them good luck in turn; and grateful when the jazz critic found a different, informed phrase of praise for each of them. Plumbers or clerks, van boys or apprentices, they were dedicated in their music, and innocent. I find it difficult across the years to explain why this word came to mind so clearly and spontaneously. For all I knew they might have been on probation or had criminal records, but their unexpressed determination to do their best would have done credit to a group of ex-public schoolboys marooned and beleaguered in darkest Africa. There was no double-take in their attitudes, and none in Mrs Forster's as she stood there meeting and greeting and encouraging – everyone. She too, big, loud and unselfconsciously vulgar, partook of this innocence.

Five minutes later we were in our places on the dais, and the leader of the club was introducing her. Amazingly, he had obtained near-silence, and by standing there next to her, assured it for Mrs Forster. She welcomed everybody, starting with the audience (which cheered itself), then the judges (spotlighted in turn, my own moment grim while my father's fame was claimed) and lastly – 'give them a really big hand' – the Ragamuffins. The first leg of the finals was under way; and my fellow judges began to fill in the pads in front of them. After a sideways glance at the TV announcer's notes, I began to follow suit.

I was going to add that 'the Ragamuffins were all right', but that cool, flat phrase is as untrue now as it was then. Much of what they played sounded like the outpourings of so many other groups; many of their effects were probably being produced in a dozen places up and down the country at that very same moment. But the sweating, strung-up intensity with which they forced themselves to give each number every ounce of drive and bounce they possessed was marvellous. They cared about the numbers and the way they projected them as if they were Beethoven's Ninth or Mahler's Second; and their sincerity seemed to reach and revitalize every boy and girl in that audience. It was with difficulty that I knocked off marks for anything; and when the Coolglos followed the Ragamuffins, the same feeling of complete integrity imposed itself on me.

Just before the shaky red curtain was pulled aside to reveal the second group, the five Ragamuffins slid from the wings down some steps and stood, backs to the wall, near the steps. They were greeted by more cheering, while two of them were joined by admiring girl-friends. All five looked hot, exhausted and nervous, yet when the curtain went up on their rivals, some of the dynamism on the stage was reflected in their expressions. It was as if they wanted to win, but only after the Coolglos had given them a close run for their money. To me this is precisely what happened, for I could see no clear differences between the two groups. The best I could do was to juggle the individual scores for musical ability, presentation and entertainment value, finishing up with the same grand total for each group.

The signalling of our marks was greeted with suffocating noise (it took more than an hour after I had left the club for the sense of that noise to leave me entirely). A long-legged, attractive blonde worked the complicated scoreboard. After ten minutes with the result in the balance, the announcement that the Coolglos had won was met with deafening cheers and cat-calls. Even the youth club leader had difficulty in securing enough calm to re-introduce Mrs Forster. Sensing that the interval of quiet was bound to be brief, she rushed off a reel of thanks, then to the sound of rising chatter, announced that the winners would be getting a recording test the following week – 'AND' (but she had them now anyway) 'it is now my great pleasure to hand them a special prize: a cheque for £50 towards buying their new equipment – from my hubby.' Now the noise of clapping and cheering, stamping and shouting, was almost unbearable; and Mrs Forster, with spotlights hugging her and ourselves bringing up the rear, was able to go back-stage to the sound of an ear-splitting ovation.

There, in a small, pale green room furnished only with a bare table and three wooden chairs, were assembled: the judges, the three youth club leaders, the A & R man, a local newspaper reporter, Mrs Forster and the Coolglos. These boys were pleased, no more, to have won; and grateful to the big, jolly woman for the prize.

But their main interest and thanks were reserved for the jazz critic, who discussed their showing bar by bar. Should that chorus have been taken faster? Did they fluff those early chords? Was the beat strong enough at the repeat? Did they really *swing*? They asked and he answered, advising, suggesting, correcting, until they seemed more contented than at any moment that evening. Then at last the leader asked him: 'Could we just do a run-through the way you says to see if we got it right?' And there was joy on their young, hot faces when he agreed, and they filed back into the hall to take over from the record player which had followed them.

The rest of the judges' party was quietly let out of the stage door. Round the back a few couples, most of them in motor-cycling gear, were necking furiously, or worse. We didn't stay to see, but hurried to the cars, leaving the jazz critic to give his final lesson. Luckily Phaedra went with her mother, so I was left with the pop singer who had had two hits in the charts.

'They was too nervous,' he explained as I resumed my convoy position. 'I've 'eard 'em do better'n that. Jimmy – 'im on lead guitar – can be fab when 'e's in the mood.'

'Do you think they'll get a recording contract?' I asked.

'Might do. Depends, see? They need a bloke taping 'em what can make them feel relaxed. The wrong sort and they're done for.' He considered the point for a further moment (or so I supposed). 'Who was that bird what you 'ad with you on the way there?'

'Mrs Forster's daughter, Phaedra.'

'Nice name,' he said dreamily. ''Ow do you spell it?'

I told him but he looked doubtful. 'I must chat 'er up when we get back. Mark you, Susie'll tear me limb from limb if I get anywhere.' And he went on to tell me about Susie and how she thought him the greatest and how his mum thought he was better than Cliff Richard ('and not just 'cause I'm 'er son') and how, if the dee-jays got it in for you, your discs didn't stand an earthly, and why Andrew Oldham thought his next one must make the top ten.

But I only half-listened. I was still overwhelmed by the sense of dedication those two groups of boys had brought to their playing. They knew all about the odds against them, the plugging and the rackets, the tremendous efforts they still had to make. But they also sensed that their integrity and ambition were a match for those odds and exploitations. They were – once more I cannot resist the word – innocents in the commercial, materialist, unscrupulous world around them. And it was this innocence that suddenly checked me in my own cynicism and disbelief.

Slightly, as I stayed through some polite drinking at Mrs Forster's, and strongly, as I drove to Hampstead, I became aware of the unfairness of the judgments I had been making. Supposing my father was right and Julian innocent? To hell with what he had written in his journal! – after all, hadn't I murdered people I loathed in my day-dreaming fantasies? He may have crazily desired but harmlessly touched the little boy, as innocent in fact as he was guilty in intention. And his defiance and self-pity afterwards may just have been a defence against our distrust and suspicion. Somehow or other on this last evening I had to show him that I, too, believed in his innocence. It was the least I could do; and it was important.

When I finally reached the flat, it was much later than I had intended. Julian was in the living-room alone, reading (to judge by the title) a novel. I managed not to ask Canter's whereabouts or what he had heard from Gater. I would let him tell me in his own time – if he wanted to. Instead, sitting on the arm of the russet-coloured couch, I told him about the contest. 'You know,' I said as I reached the moment when we left the club, 'nine-tenths of the pop game is sticky and dirty. The stuff they write and play is corny and shallow. The plugging of it to the kids is as commercial as you can get; and every bit of the industry is aimed at the lowest common denominator. And yet *these* kids are as innocent as a spring morning.'

Julian smiled vaguely. Had I bored him? Did he think that I had been sold an act that was as tainted as any branch of the industry? Then suddenly I knew, knew as I watched his slightly jerky movements and syrupy grin that he was drunk, or as near as doesn't matter. He had been sitting there alone, reading and quietly knocking back whisky, and was now enveloped in the sort of euphoria that left him pleasantly touched by my story. Good for him, then! He was entitled to a few hours escape if anyone was. I refilled his glass for him without even waiting to be asked; and he looked delighted.

We sat in silence then for some long minutes. The rather ugly
wooden clock on the mantelpiece ticked solemnly, cars passed in
the street outside and Julian's breathing became audible, almost
laboured. Something heavy was dropped on the floor above and a
dog started barking. 'They're going on with the charge,' Julian said
without abandoning his fixed smile. 'Indecent assault. It covers a
multitude of sins, committed and omitted.' He sipped his drink
like a wine connoisseur tasting a new vintage. 'Roy Gater's confident we'll win.'

'I agree with every word mother said as she was leaving this
afternoon.' I spoke and felt awkwardly. To emphasize my belief in
him, I crossed the room and put my hand on his shoulder. 'You'll
be all right,' I said with a wink, 'it's just a bit of beastly luck.'

What happened then took a minute, half a minute, ten seconds.
My anger was so sharp and violent that time exploded in its wake,
and I lost track of it. At one instant I stood there, hand on Julian's
shoulder, feeling desperately sorry for the good, kind man who
had slipped up – *if* he had. At the next my slimy, crawling uncle
had unhooked my zip and slid his hand into my crutch. He said
something but I didn't want to hear it. I sloshed him, or meant to
or thought I did. Recoiling, I ran out of the room and house, down
the steps and into the car, starting, twisting and turning it away
from the kerb almost before the door was shut.

'DAVID!'

His shout split the night air like a shot. But I was away, aware
of Julian at the door, of the gathering speed of the car, of the
snow-balling hate for him which grew with every revolution of
the wheels.

twenty

THE rest is epilogue. The few people to whom I have talked intimately over the years feel that I have told enough; some among them would even have me maintain complete silence. Against this there are the rumours, appearing in all sorts of likely and unlikely places, magnified, distorted, damaging. Besides, if you have borne with me this far, I owe *you* the duty of completing the story. You may know what happened to my father, probably do; but where are Julian and Canter now? Or Molly and Karen? Where, in another sense, am I?

I shall answer the last question first, because *au fond* this story is *my* justification. Had I written it two, three or five years ago, I would have ended with Julian's great, appealing 'DAVID!' I might not, even then, have emerged as a hero, or *l'homme moyen sensuel* with a little of the 'English gentleman' stirred in. Now, I feel the need to press the last piece into place, changing the whole portrait in the process. I can do it because at last it is a part of the past; because my wife knows and encourages me in the step I am taking. Yet to this day I wish I had driven straight home that night, put away the car and quietly made my way to bed. A good night's sleep and a few early morning hours of reflection might have swung the balance. As it was I stopped the car at the first call box I came to and dialled the Belgravia number.

My father answered. Do you believe in signs, portents and omens? If so, this was one. As a first line of defence against the press and others, my father almost never answered the telephone. Most often it was the maid, occasionally my mother, who enquired the caller's name and purpose before committing father to being at home. 'Yes, David?'

'You know my chest of drawers opposite the window? You know, by the door?'

'Yes.'

'Go to the bottom drawer and slip your hand into the shirts. You'll find a parcel hidden there. Open it and read.'

'What's this all about?'

'Julian.'

'Surely you can give me some indication of the reason for all this mystery?'

I looked up to the mirror over the coin box. Someone was waiting to use the box. My father was still talking, but I quietly replaced the receiver and stepped outside. I drove to town, parked the car and went to the Percolator. Did I still hope to see Karen after all the humiliation of our last meeting? Or to increase that humiliation by bumping into Martin? But neither were there, nor was there anyone else I knew. So I quietly downed cup after cup of coffee and watched the strangers round me without ever really seeing them. And all the time I played and replayed *the* scene, adding endless details from the past seen through the prism of my new and horrifying awareness. Whatever decision my father might take on reading that journal would never be punishment enough for that revolting pervert. And this mood stayed with me through the night which I spent in a cheap Bloomsbury hotel.

When I reached home next morning, my parents were extravagantly sympathetic. I was treated like a returning soldier who has been away for years on active service. Nor was anything said on the subject of Julian. As far as I was concerned they had read the journal, knew every last loathsome detail and were acting accordingly. Right through the twice postponed trial, the actual hearing and the quick, unfortunate consequences, I acted on that assumption. Months, in fact, went by before I knew that the parcel had never been opened. A quarter of an hour after *my* call, had come one from Julian. Hearing that I was not there, he gave a muffled account of the incident blaming everything on the drink. Although shocked, father told him of my call, adding that even at that moment the parcel lay unopened on his desk. Julian's response was unequivocal. 'Cut me off, cut me out of your life completely, do what you like but burn that parcel I beg of you.' My father, of course, did so.

At the third hearing the case was proceeded with. Julian was represented by a Stratford solicitor, Gater having long since withdrawn on my father's instructions. It made the *Evening Standard*; it made *The News of the World*; and in each case Julian's relationship to my father was underlined. Was it this or was there a more straight-forward piece of political double-crossing? Those in the know differ diametrically. The simple fact is that Bradley became Prime Minister and my father stayed on at the Ministry of Communications. Most political commentators expressed their surprise but added that it could only be a matter of time before he was promoted. We hardly discussed it at home but I suspect that my father knew that he was out of the main race – for ever.

Karen never married Martin Bensted, though I was not to learn the reason. A few months after I had left Hampstead she even rang me at home, but I had already moved to digs. By the end of my second year at the College I was again on formal talking terms with Grant Dellon. He still had a gossip's reputation, so I asked him for news of her. But he either knew nothing or wanted to be mysterious to increase his sense of importance: 'you'd better get that from someone else,' he answered darkly. I probably annoyed him by not pressing the point.

Martin and I never went further than nodding good-morning; and when, at the end of the second year, we moved into different departments, the need for this rarely arose. I think I once heard that after College he went into an advertising agency, married a very luscious piece and lived moderately unhappily ever after. But perhaps I am confusing him with someone else.

I never saw Molly again. Cutting myself off from Julian ensured that, for she remained absolutely loyal to him. When he resigned his partnership and left the Stock Exchange, Lance found him a reasonable job in his own firm; and Julian's been there ever since. I don't think the slightly inconclusive trial (he was found guilty, but only just, to judge from the magistrate's comments) caused him more than temporary anguish. The fine, certainly, was only a sharp pinprick; the probation somewhat more humiliating, and irritating as well.

Once more I am tempted to stop at this point; once more some-thing drives me to record the last detail. Is this, perhaps, a vicious streak in me? Or just the less reprehensible desire to add: 'I told

you so!'? For Canter, whom I had never liked or trusted, walked
out on Julian just after the case was heard. It's a long time since
I saw his name in any West End cast list, though occasionally he
does get bit parts on television.

Julian came to lunch with us two Sundays ago. When my wife
was putting the children into the garden after lunch, I taxed him
about the actor. It was the first time reference had been made
to the subject in years, but he heard my question and comment
calmly. 'You know, David, you're quite wrong. He was, and I think
is, very fond of me. But he met someone while I was in Stratford
over that trial business and fell head over heels in love with him.
And Canter's particular sort of moral honesty would never let him
deceive me or reduce me to the status of a number two. For that
reason he *had* to go.'

It's a strange world, isn't it? Julian obviously believed every word
he was saying.

ALSO AVAILABLE FROM VALANCOURT BOOKS

C.H.B. KITCHIN	Ten Pollitt Place
	The Book of Life
HILDA LEWIS	The Witch and the Priest
KENNETH MARTIN	Aubade
MICHAEL MCDOWELL	The Amulet
	The Elementals
MICHAEL NELSON	Knock or Ring
	A Room in Chelsea Square
BEVERLEY NICHOLS	Crazy Pavements
OLIVER ONIONS	The Hand of Kornelius Voyt
J.B. PRIESTLEY	Benighted
	The Doomsday Men
	The Other Place
	The Magicians
	Saturn Over the Water
PETER PRINCE	Play Things
PIERS PAUL READ	Monk Dawson
FORREST REID	Following Darkness
	The Spring Song
	Brian Westby
	The Tom Barber Trilogy
	Denis Bracknel
GEORGE SIMS	Sleep No More
	The Last Best Friend
ANDREW SINCLAIR	The Facts in the Case of E.A. Poe
	The Raker
COLIN SPENCER	Panic
DAVID STOREY	Radcliffe
	Pasmore
	Saville
RUSSELL THORNDIKE	The Slype
	The Master of the Macabre
JOHN TREVENA	Sleeping Waters
JOHN WAIN	Hurry on Down
	The Smaller Sky
	Strike the Father Dead
	A Winter in the Hills
KEITH WATERHOUSE	There is a Happy Land
	Billy Liar
COLIN WILSON	Ritual in the Dark
	Man Without a Shadow
	The Philosopher's Stone
	The God of the Labyrinth